It Wasn't Supposed To Be Like This.

From what Ryan had been told, Julie Nelson was a gold-digging bimbo who needed a good lesson. And he'd been just the man to volunteer to teach it. He'd expected her to be a vapid, overaccessorized man-eater. Instead he'd found a beautiful, intelligent, sincere woman who made him laugh and believe in possibilities again.

Right now he should be feeling like he'd done the world a favor. But he'd just created a hell of a mess, and had no idea how to fix it.

He liked Julie. *A lot.*

How was he going to explain that he wasn't Todd Aston III—and that she'd just been set up to take a fall?

Dear Reader,

One of my favorite things to write about is finding family. It's a constant theme for me and this series is no exception. While my three heroines, Julie, Willow and Marina, already have a great family, they've recently discovered a long-lost grandmother who very much wants to be a part of their lives.

Grandma Ruth isn't exactly the cookie-baking type. Instead she's elegant, sophisticated and rich. She also has a nephew by marriage she adores. She decides everything would be perfect if only one of her granddaughters would marry her favorite nephew-by-marriage. To entice the girls, she offers them each a million dollars if one of them will say, "I do."

Our heroines are both shocked and intrigued. It kind of is a lot of money. But marriage? To a perfect stranger? Well, maybe if *he* were perfect…

Welcome to THE MILLION DOLLAR CATCH, where nothing is what it seems and falling in love is a whole lot more complicated than anyone ever imagined.

Susan Mallery

SUSAN MALLERY

THE SUBSTITUTE MILLIONAIRE

Published by Silhouette Books
America's Publisher of Contemporary Romance

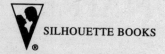

SILHOUETTE BOOKS

ISBN-13: 978-0-373-76760-1
ISBN-10:   0-373-76760-9

THE SUBSTITUTE MILLIONAIRE

Copyright © 2006 by Susan Macias Redmond

SUSAN MALLERY

is the bestselling and award-winning author of over fifty books for Harlequin Books and Silhouette Books. She makes her home in Los Angeles with her handsome prince of a husband and her two adorable-but-not-bright cats.

One

Julie Nelson's first blind date had gone so badly, she'd sworn off them for the next ten years.

The guy in question had flirted with every female *but* her at the all-you-can-eat buffet, double-dipped in their shared bowl of salad dressing and then skipped out on the bill, leaving her to pay and get herself home. She'd been sixteen and if she hadn't ended up in the emergency room with a horrible case of food poisoning, she might have been able to put the night behind her.

But throwing up all over the only cute intern had been the last straw. She'd vowed never again, for any reason imaginable in this lifetime or any to follow, to *ever* go on another blind date.

Until tonight.

"This is going to be a disaster," she muttered to

herself as she handed her car keys to the valet and made her way to the front of a trendy west side restaurant. "I'm smarter than this. What on earth am I doing here?"

Dumb question, when she already knew the answer. She and her two sisters had been faced with a choice of who got the first shot at dating the infamous Todd Aston III. Their time-honored tradition of making all of life's truly important decisions with a rousing round of Rock, Paper, Scissors had left Julie the loser, and therefore the date. She was a sucker for the scissors and her sisters knew it.

She pulled open the sleek glass door and stepped into the crowded foyer. Apparently tables at this place were as hard to come by as free parking. She wove through the well-dressed crowd until she faced a very young, very thin, very pale hostess.

"I'm meeting Todd Aston," Julie said as she fought against the need to tell the girl that a sandwich wouldn't kill her.

The young woman glanced down at her reservation book. "Mr. Aston is already here. I'll show you to his table."

Julie followed the waif to the rear of the restaurant, trying not to compare her own size-normal hips to the nonexistent ones in front of her. Although feeling inadequate was actually more fun than sweating a meeting with Todd Aston III. How did anyone live with a number after his name? It made her think of Mr. Howell on *Gilligan's Island*, a late-night favorite when she'd been growing up.

She instantly pictured a younger version of Mr.

Howell, complete with striped slacks and a white blazer
and was fighting the need to laugh when the hostess
stopped in front of a table tucked in the corner and
pointed to someone who very definitely did *not* look
like an aging, pretentious millionaire.

Todd Aston stood and smiled. "Hello. You must be
Julie."

Losing Rock, Paper, Scissors had never looked so
good, she thought as she took in the fact that he towered
over her despite the dangerously high heels she wore.
Todd was *handsome* with dark eyes and a smile that
reminded her just a little of the one Big Bad Wolf must
have given Red Riding Hood.

He didn't look nerdy, desperate or inbred—and she
had a feeling he wouldn't be sticking her with the bill.

"Hi, Todd," she said. "Good to meet you."

He held out her chair, which was a nice and unexpected touch, then moved back to his seat. The hostess
left them alone.

She studied him, taking in the dark hair, the hint of
a dimple on his left cheek and the subtle power tie that
had probably cost as much as her last student-loan
payment.

"So, this is awkward," she said cheerfully, deciding
there was no point in ignoring the obvious.

His left eyebrow rose. "No social niceties where we
ask about the weather and how the traffic was on the
drive over?"

"Sure, if you'd prefer. The weather is beautiful, but
hey, it's Southern California and we expect that. As for
the traffic, it was fine. And your day?"

He smiled again. "You're not what I expected."

She could only imagine what that would have been. "I'm not too young, too plastic and too desperate?"

He winced. "Again the lack of social niceties. Whatever would your mother say?"

Julie considered the question. "Only have one glass of wine, make sure that he's nice and if you like him, give him your number."

He laughed. The sound was low and rich and masculine. So far she'd been existing on nerves and sheer bravado, but when his smile turned into a grin, she felt the tiniest quiver somewhere behind her belly button.

Interesting. Maybe she should have given this blind-date thing a second chance a whole lot sooner.

"That's good advice," he said. "I think I like your mother."

"She's worth liking."

The waiter appeared and handed them menus, then asked for their drink orders. Todd chose an eighteen-year-old Scotch while Julie ordered a vodka tonic.

"Not following Mom's advice?" he asked when the waiter had left.

"It's been a long day."

"Doing what?"

"I'm a second-year associate at an international law firm."

"A lawyer. Pass the bar yet?"

"Of course."

He chuckled. "You sound confident."

"Confidence comes easily after the fact."

"And before?"

"Eighteen-hour workdays *and* studying. It made for a full life."

"What kind of international law? Human rights, that sort of thing?"

"*Corporate* international law," she told him. "I specialize in contracts and associations with China."

"Interesting specialty."

She loved being underestimated, especially by a man. "It was a natural fit for me. I speak Mandarin."

He was good. He only looked a little shocked and then quickly recovered. "Impressive."

"Thank you."

His gaze sharpened slighted as he studied her. "Okay, I think we should start over."

She laughed. "Why? Things are going so well."

"Sure. For you. Look, I was told by my aunt Ruth that there was a 'young lady' she wanted me to meet. I was given a time and a place and I'm here. I was expecting someone…different. You're a nice surprise."

She let her gaze linger on his broad shoulders. Either he worked out or he came from a very fine gene pool. Actually, she could accept either.

"Do you always do what Aunt Ruth says?"

"Most of the time." He shrugged. "She's really my great-great-aunt or something. But she's good to me and I care about her. She doesn't ask me much so if it's important to her, I try to say yes. This was important."

Either he was telling the truth, or he was really, really good with his lines. Right then, she wanted him to be sincere.

"You're a good surprise, too," she admitted, deciding

to trust him for now. "When I walked in, I was picturing Mr. Howell."

"From *Gilligan's Island?* Thanks."

Laughing, she asked, "Would you rather be Gilligan?"

"I'd rather be James Bond."

"You're not British."

"I can work on the accent."

She leaned toward him. "So is it the gadgets or the women that make James Bond so appealing?"

"Both."

"You're being honest."

"You sound surprised."

She was. "I can adjust," she said. "Okay, James-slash-Todd, all I know about you is you dress like a businessman and you adore your aunt Ruth. Well, and the whole number-after-your-name thing, but we probably shouldn't get into that."

"What's wrong with the number after my name?"

"Nothing. It's lovely. I always have to skip over that box when I'm registering on Internet sites, but you get to stop and put in a big three."

"The three isn't actually that big. It's the same size as all the other numbers. It wants to be big, of course, but unfulfilled fantasies are a reality of life. Three has to get used to that."

Charming, she thought happily. The man was completely charming.

The waiter appeared with their drinks. When he'd left, Todd held up his glass.

"To the unexpected pleasure of a smart, funny, beautiful woman," he said.

Okay, *that* was a line, but she was having enough fun that she would accept it in the spirit she hoped he meant it.

"Thank you." She touched her glass to his.

Somehow she misjudged and their fingers brushed. It was nothing—a brief, meaningless bit of contact. But she was oddly aware of it. Her sister Willow would tell her it was the universe giving her a message and that she should listen to it. Her sister Marina would want to know if Todd was "the one."

"So what do *you* do?" she asked.

He set down his glass. "I skywrite. You know, those horrible messages people are always leaving each other in the clouds. Barney Loves Cathy. John, Bring Home Milk."

She took another sip of her drink and waited.

He sighed. "I'm a partner in a venture capital firm. We buy into small businesses, shower them with money and expertise until they're big companies, then sell them to someone else and make an obscene amount of profit. It's disgusting. I should be ashamed."

She laughed. "I would have thought you'd be running the family foundation."

"There's a professional board that takes care of that. I'd rather build than give away."

"Sounds ruthless," she teased.

"I can be. Very. People tend to underestimate me because of the number after my name. They assume I'm useless. I'm not."

She believed him. Funny, powerful and very easy to look at. Especially now, when he stared at her so intently. She sensed she had his full attention—which was both thrilling and a little scary.

"But then they underestimate you, too," he added.

"You know this how?"

"Because I did. I assumed human-rights law when you said you were working internationally."

"It's a guy thing," she said. "The assumption that women will go for emotion rather than business."

"You get that a lot." He wasn't asking a question.

"Yes, but I don't mind. I use it. My career is very important to me. The first few years in a big law firm can be tough. I want to get ahead, but I was raised to do the right thing. So I'll take the advantage of being underestimated and run with it."

"Ruthless?" he asked.

"I flirt with ruthless, but we've never actually been a couple."

Their gazes locked. Until that moment, Julie had been enjoying her drink and the company, but suddenly tension crackled around them. She felt the hairs on the back of her neck prickle. She'd thought Todd would be prissy and he'd thought she would be an idiot. Instead she found herself rethinking her plan of no involvements until after her second year at the law firm ended. While she didn't have a lot of spare time, with the right incentive, she could make an exception.

She liked that he was smart and cynical and still paid attention to what his aunt Ruth had to say. She liked his smile and the interest flickering in his dark eyes.

For the first time in a really long time, she felt a

warmth between her thighs. Good to know that part of her wasn't completely dead.

"Tell me about the women in your life," she said.

He'd been drinking and nearly choked. "I didn't bring pictures."

"That's all right. A brief overview is plenty. I'll pass on the résumés this time."

"You're so generous." He set down his glass. "There were the twins…"

She smiled. "You don't do twins and I don't scare that easily."

"All right. No one serious at the moment." He frowned. "Make that no one at the moment. A difficult breakup last year. No ex-wives, no ex-fiancées. You?"

"One ex-fiancé from my last year of law school. No one now."

"What happened to the fool?"

Julie might not be on the dating circuit, but she knew when to sidestep a topic. There was no point in getting into her sad little story. "Things didn't work out."

The waiter appeared and asked if they had any questions about the menu.

"As that would have required us to look at them," Todd said as he grinned at her, "not yet. But we'll work on it."

Julie waited until they were alone and said, "Why bother with a menu? You're going to order steak, close to rare, and a salad. Not because you want one, but because if you don't eat a vegetable, people will think you weren't raised right."

He raised his left eyebrow. "You'll want the steak,

but there's the whole 'women don't eat on dates' thing, so you'll get fish, which you don't really like." He picked up his glass. "I take that back. You do like fish—but only in a beer batter, deep fried, with fries on the side."

"I like tuna," she said primly.

"Something from a can doesn't count."

She laughed. "All right, you win. I'll get the steak and even eat it, but you can't tell."

"Fair enough. And I'll order the damn salad." He leaned toward her. His dark gaze locked on hers. "I expected to be bored."

"Me, too. I also thought I'd feel morally and intellectually superior."

He grinned. "I'm comfortable with the moral superiority."

"But I can't be smarter?"

"I'm a pretty smart guy."

She shifted in her seat as the temperature in the room seemed to climb about sixteen degrees.

She reached for her drink, but before she could pick it up, he captured her hand in his. His fingers were warm and strong as he rubbed her knuckles. Jolts of awareness moved up her arm and from there zipped to all sorts of interesting places in her body. She felt languid and wholly feminine—an unusual combination for her. Normally she went for in charge and intimidating.

"I have a technical question," he said as he shifted his hand so his thumb could rub against the center of her palm. "It's about my aunt Ruth."

"Which is?"

"She's your grandmother."

"That's the rumor," Julie said, trying to keep her mind on the conversation rather than getting lost in the need stealing through her. She told herself her reaction to Todd was more about the fact that she hadn't been on a date in over eighteen months than anything he was doing. The problem was, she couldn't seem to convince herself.

"If she's my great-aunt and your grandmother," he said. "That makes us…"

Ah, okay. She understood his concern. "Unrelated. She was your great-uncle's second wife. They didn't have any children together. She made it a point to explain all that. She didn't tell you?"

He withdrew his hand and sat up. "No. She didn't."

"Now you know." Speaking of Grandmother Ruth, Julie was going to have to send her a big thank-you when she got home.

"Now, I do." He stood and held out his hand to her.

"What are you doing?" she asked.

"Inviting you to dance."

Dance? As in…dance? She hadn't done that since high school, and even then she hadn't been very good.

"They don't have dancing here," she said, staying firmly in her seat.

"Of course they do. And now that I know we're not cousins, let's dance."

She was torn between the fear of making a fool out of herself and the thrill of pressing her body against his. Because now that she'd bothered to notice, she could hear soft, slow music in the background. It sounded nice, but it wasn't nearly as tempting as the man standing in front of her.

"Are you going to make me beg?" he asked.

"Would you?"

One corner of his mouth turned up in a smile. "Maybe."

She rose and put her hand in his. He led her to the rear of the restaurant, where a three-piece combo played and several couples clung to each other on the small dance floor.

Before she could get her bearings, Todd pulled her against him and put his free hand on her waist. She found herself resting her fingers on his shoulder.

He was all hard, lean muscle, she thought as her thighs brushed against his. They weren't close enough for her breasts to brush against his chest, but she had a sudden wild and inappropriate desire to lean in and rub…like a lonely cat.

Too long without a man, she told herself. And wasn't this a really inconvenient time to figure that out?

"You smell good," he murmured in her ear.

"Copier toner," she whispered back. "Do you like it? I had to change the cartridge today."

He groaned. "Can't you take the compliment?"

"All right. Thank you."

"Better." He smiled at her. "You're not easy."

"Now that's a compliment I can get behind."

"You like being difficult?"

"Sometimes. Don't you?"

He moved his hand from her waist to the small of her back. "Sometimes," he said, echoing her answer.

She looked into his eyes. "You don't like people making assumptions about you."

"You made them."

"You made them as well. We're even."

"More than even, Julie. We're good."

With that, he lowered his head and lightly brushed her mouth with his. The kiss was unexpected but delicious. Her stomach clenched and her breasts began to ache. He moved back and forth, but didn't deepen the kiss.

Public place, she told herself. He didn't want to embarrass her. She should appreciate that. And she would…in time.

He straightened, then cleared his throat. "We should probably go back and order dinner. You know, be responsible."

For a heartbeat, she almost asked about the alternative. What would happen if they kept dancing and touching and kissing? Except she kind of had a feeling she knew the answer to the question.

Too much, too soon, she told herself as they stepped apart. She hadn't been doing the dating thing for a long time—taking it slow made a lot of sense. But the man did tempt her.

He kept her hand in his as they walked back to their table.

"You never told me why you're here," he said when they were seated. "I told you Aunt Ruth asked me to come. What's your excuse?"

He didn't know? Seriously? Oh, my. This could be good.

"My mother and her mother have been estranged for years. Ruth popped back into our lives a couple of months ago. My sisters and I had never met her before. Mom hadn't even mentioned her. Last week, at dinner, Ruth said she had a great nephew and suggested one of us go out with you."

"Interesting."

"More than interesting. She offered us...it's not important."

"Of course it is."

"You'll be insulted."

"I can handle the truth," he teased. "What did she offer?"

"Money."

He stared at her. "She's paying you to date me?"

"Oh, no. The dates are free. Now if I marry you, I get cash. A million dollars. Each. For me, my sisters and my mom. Pretty cool, huh."

A muscle in his jaw twitched, but otherwise, he didn't show any emotion. She couldn't begin to imagine what he was thinking.

"We were all surprised," Julie said. "We couldn't figure out what could possibly be so wrong with you that your aunt had to offer that kind of money to get someone to marry you."

"Wrong? With me?"

"Sure."

She was enjoying herself, but trying really hard to keep him from knowing.

"We decided that one of us would go on a date and figure out how truly awful you were," she continued.

"We played Rock, Paper, Scissors to determine the most likely candidate."

He actually flinched at that. "Rock, Paper..." He cleared his throat. "So you won."

She allowed herself to smile. "Oh, no, Todd. I lost."

Two

The waiter arrived to take their order. Julie placed hers, then waited while Todd did the same. He barely glanced at the menu, instead keeping his gaze fixed on her.

"You lost?" he asked, his voice slightly strangled. "As in, you didn't win?"

She allowed herself a small smile. "Uh-huh. You know how it goes. The loser has to do the icky thing. That would be this date with you. Total ick."

"You lost?"

He seemed unable to comprehend the fact that the three of them hadn't been dying to be his lady for the night. Ah, the foolishness of men.

"If it makes you feel any better," she said before taking a sip of her drink. "I'm glad I lost."

"I can't tell you how that confession moves me."

"You shouldn't take it so hard. Look at the situation from our perspective. Your own great-aunt, who has known you all your life, is willing to pay a woman to marry you. We figured at the very least you had a hump on your back and maybe some odd disease that left you twisted and bumpy. Like the Elephant Man."

He nearly choked on his drink. "You thought I was the Elephant Man?"

"It was a consideration. And yet I showed up anyway."

"You lost and I'm a mercy date. Great. I can't believe Ruth offered you a million dollars."

She thought that was odd, too, but hey, everyone had strange relatives. "Not for the date. Remember? The date is free. I have a really simple solution to the problem—don't propose."

He grinned. "Oh, sure. Easy for you to say, but now I don't have any entertainment for the dessert course."

As she laughed, she admitted to herself that he was nothing like she'd imagined. Anyone with a number after his name had to be stuffy and he wasn't. She liked him—a lot.

"You should have gotten something for the date," he told her. "Fifty thousand, at least."

"You know, I didn't even think of that. But if Grandmother Ruth mentions it again, I get a check."

He gazed into her eyes. "I'm glad you lost, too."

"Thank you. Although my losing wasn't hard to predict. I'm kind of a sucker for scissor and my sisters know. So someone is always playing the rock."

"Interesting way to determine your destiny."

She raised her eyebrows. "Destiny? Are you implying you're mine?"

She expected him to squirm, but he shrugged. "Neither of us thought things would go this well. Maybe fate had a hand in tonight."

She groaned. "No talk of fate or the universe, I beg you. My sister Willow is constantly explaining how each of us has a destiny we can't escape. She's very sweet and I love her to death, but sometimes I want to choke her. Plus, if you could see the things she eats…sprouts and tofu and slimy drinks." Julie shuddered.

He nodded sympathetically. "Vegetarian?"

"Most of the time. Although she has an entire list of foods that don't count as meat. Like hamburgers at a picnic or hot dogs at a Dodger game."

"Interesting."

"She's great. Marina is, too. She's the baby of the family. Just think, you could have been out with either of them."

"I'm happy with the sister I have."

"But you don't have me." Although he certainly could, she thought wistfully, remembering how she'd felt his in arms.

"Give me time."

Julie glanced in her rearview mirror for the hundredth time in the past seven minutes. Dinner had been fabulous. She couldn't remember a thing about the food, although she was confident that had been great. It was the conversation she remembered. The sexy banter, the laughter—the connection.

She couldn't remember the last time a man had pulled her in so completely. One minute she'd been dreading the evening and the next she'd wanted to stop time so it would never end.

Todd was amazing. Funny and smart and he got her humor, which didn't always happen. And the physical chemistry...he could make her melt just by looking at her.

All of which was really nice, but was she prepared to take things where they were obviously headed? His offer to follow her home to make sure she arrived safely was a very thin disguise for what he was really offering—naked Todd in her bed.

The question wasn't if she wanted that—she did with a desperation that left her hungry and restless. It wasn't about wanting, it was about being sensible. She hadn't had a man in her life since Garrett. Not that she was going to think about that lying bastard right now. The point was, she hadn't been playing the dating game for a long time. She was out of practice. Sure, tonight had gone well, but did that mean she should celebrate by inviting Todd in and having her way with him?

She still hadn't decided when they arrived at her place. She pulled in front of the single-car garage and climbed out of her car. The night was still and clear, not too cold because even though it was fall, it was still Los Angeles where real weather need not apply.

Nerves tingled and danced throughout her body. Every cell from her ears down begged her to take the very handsome and capable man up on his yet-to-be-made offer. Her skin ached to be touched and her feminine bits could use with a good ravishing. But her brain warned her to be careful. Sure, Todd was all things charming, but what did she really know about him? Besides, sex on the first date was so tacky.

He parked on the street and climbed out, then glanced around.

"Not what I expected," he said quietly as he approached. "I thought you'd live in something new and shiny."

The neighborhood was older, with a lot of houses having been converted into duplexes. Julie liked the settled atmosphere of the neighborhood and craftsman details inside and out.

"I'm close to work and I get to have a bit of grass," she said. "I'm not really a condo person."

He smiled down at her, then brushed her cheek with his thumb. "Good thing we didn't go to my place."

"Let me guess. It's all glass and steel."

"That, too, but mostly because it's farther."

With that, he kissed her.

His mouth was warm and firm, yet gentle. He moved slowly, as if he had all the time in the world, and she liked that. She liked how he put his hands on her waist and didn't grab for anything significant.

She stepped in a little closer and rested her fingers on his shoulders. Thank goodness her purse had a long strap, so she didn't have to waste time holding it. She wanted to have the freedom to explore his arms and back.

He was all hard muscles through the well-tailored fabric of his suit. He was also warm and alive and just tall enough that even in her heels she had to stretch a little to keep their mouths connected.

She definitely wanted the kiss to continue. Even without him deepening it, she felt tingles in all the right places and a few that surprised her. Her chest was tight, her legs kind of trembly and she had the sudden thought she was never going to be able to catch her breath again.

He drifted slightly, kissed her cheek, then along her jaw. Little brushing touches of lips on sensitized skin. He nipped her earlobe, which made her jump and shiver and need, then lightly touched the tip of his tongue to the side of her neck.

Goose bumps broke out all over. She gasped as heat poured through her. The wanting overwhelmed her until she knew that she couldn't possibly survive another second if he didn't kiss her. Really kiss her.

Fortunately Todd seemed to be a good mind reader. He brought his mouth back to hers. She parted her lips and he plunged inside of her, as if his need to take was as great as her desire to be taken.

She met him stroke for stroke, savoring the passion flaring between them. Even as his tongue mated with hers, he dropped his hands to her hips and pulled her close. She arched against him.

Two thoughts struck her at once. That the pressure of her swollen, sensitive breasts against his chest was wonderful torture, and that he was rock hard.

Images filled her brain—of them naked, touching, him filling her. She was dying from hunger and that hunger made her frantic. She tried to battle her body's desire for a man she barely knew, but it was like trying to herd cats—pointless and a little silly.

He pulled back a little and cupped her face. "This is

where I'm supposed to offer to leave," he said as he stared into her eyes. "It's how I was raised and the polite thing to do."

"Good manners are important," she murmured, pleased that she was able to speak at all. She'd wondered if it was possible, what with how every nerve was on fire.

"I agree." He drew in a ragged breath. "There is also an alternative option."

"Bad manners?"

He grinned, then lightly kissed her. "I want you, Julie. I can give you a list of really good reasons why this is a bad idea, but I want you. Desperately."

She'd never made a man desperate before, she thought as the ache between her legs grew.

"Good manners, a witty conversationalist and a great kisser," she whispered. "Who could refuse that?"

"Not me."

"Me, either."

She pulled her keys out of her purse and led the way to the front door. With each step, she braced herself for second or even third thoughts. Instead there was only a pounding rhythm urging her to hurry.

Once inside, she set her keys and her purse on the small table by the door. Todd shrugged out of what she would guess was a very expensive jacket and let it fall to the floor. Then he pulled her against him and kissed her with a thoroughness that left her weak and made her wonder how intensely he would do other things.

She kissed him just as deeply, running her hands over his chest, feeling the slick silk of his tie and the smooth cotton of his shirt. He slid one hand down to her rear, where he squeezed, and moved the other hand up until he cupped her breast.

Even through the fabric of her dress and her bra, she felt his strong fingers exploring, teasing, caressing. He lingered on her tight nipple, brushing back and forth until she wanted to rip off her clothes so he could touch her bare skin.

He nudged her backward. She reached for his tie and managed to pull it free, then she started on the buttons of his shirt. He fumbled for the zipper at the back of her dress.

They made it into the hall. She'd left a light on in the living room, but here it was dark. He kissed his way down her neck, his warm mouth making her moan. Tingles and shivers and ripples overtook her. Hunger consumed.

He made his way to the vee of her dress and his mouth settled on the curve of her breast. At the same time she found the hall light switch and he tugged down her zipper. The light came on in time for her to see as well as feel her dress fall to the floor. Todd's dark, passion-filled gaze locked with hers as he closed both hands over her breasts.

"You're beautiful," he murmured. "Hot and soft and I don't care if it *is* copier toner, you smell great."

She laughed and moaned at the same time as he rubbed her nipples. Her entire body tightened as her swollen, damp center cried out for some attention of its own.

Still touching her breasts, he leaned in for another kiss. She welcomed him, closing her lips around his tongue and sucking until he, too, shuddered.

Suddenly this wasn't enough. She wanted more—all. She wanted the weight of him on top of her. She wanted him filling her over and over again until she had no choice but to give herself up to the pleasure of her orgasm.

"Clothes," she said against his mouth. "You're wearing too many."

"Good point."

As he shrugged out of his shirt, she stepped over her dress and led the way into her small bedroom. The light from the hall was more than enough for what they were going to do. She turned to face him, only to find him staring at her.

"What?"

He swore softly. "Are you trying to kill me? You're a walking, breathing fantasy. Do the partners at your law firm know what you wear under your suits?"

She glanced down at the matching pink bra and bikini panties. They were a little lacy, but nothing special. She'd bought them on sale, but hey, guys were easy.

"They probably suspect I'm wearing underwear," she murmured as she stepped out of her high heels. "I'd rather they thought that than speculated about me wearing nothing at all. That would be tacky."

The appreciation in his gaze made her bold. Or maybe it was the fact that Todd was a sure thing that gave her confidence. Either way she slid one strap off her shoulder and smiled.

"Did you want me to take this off?"

He'd already kicked off his shoes and was in the process of lowering his slacks. As she spoke, his erection actually pulsed. She saw it through his dark briefs.

He swallowed. "That would be great."

His slacks dropped to the ground, pooling at his ankles. He didn't seem to notice. Instead his gaze fixed on her chest.

She reached behind her and unfastened her bra, then tossed it toward the dresser.

She had no idea if it actually made it because she was too caught up in the expression on Todd's face. Wonder and desire blended in a look so passionate and male that it took her breath away.

She'd been with men before and she'd been reasonably certain that they'd wanted her. After all, there had been obvious proof. But Todd stared at her as if she were his last meal. His appreciation made her feel special and exotic and more than anxious to make all his dreams come true.

He moved toward her and nearly stumbled as he got caught in his slacks. "I'm totally smooth," he muttered as he freed himself, then pulled off his socks.

She thought about mentioning the fact that she *liked* that he wasn't perfect. It made him seem more approachable somehow. But then he was pulling her close and touching her and speaking became a highly overrated activity.

His hands were everywhere—her arms, her stomach, then he cupped her bare breasts. He didn't kiss her as he explored her curves, then lightly touched her nipples with his fingers. Instead he stared into her eyes and she found herself very close to begging to be taken.

She held his gaze as long as she could, but soon sensation overwhelmed her. If was as if there were a direct line of pleasure from her breasts to between her legs. With each touch, both became more needy.

"Todd," she whispered, hoping she didn't sound as desperate as she felt.

He nudged her backward until she felt the bed behind her. Then he wrapped his arms around her, turned and lowered them both onto the mattress.

She landed on him, her legs spread, her center nestled on his arousal. He smiled up at her.

"Now I have you exactly where I want you," he whispered. "In my power."

"I'm on top," she told him. "I'm in charge."

"Wanna bet?"

He put his hands on her hips and urged her back and forth. Even through the layers of her panties and his briefs, she felt the delicious heat and friction. With a groan, she gave herself up to the sensation. It was nearly enough to get her over the edge.

"Just that like," he murmured as he began to touch her breasts.

The combination of sensations was unbelievably sensual. Tension tightened all her muscles as she felt herself racing closer and closer to her release.

Not like this, she thought frantically. Not so quickly. Not while still wearing clothes. But she also couldn't stop rubbing faster and faster.

Without warning, he rolled them both onto their sides. He removed her panties with one smooth, practiced move, then pulled off his briefs. Before she had a chance to check things out, she was on her back and his mouth was on her left breast.

He sucked and licked and teased until she thought she would go crazy from the pleasure. At the same time, he slipped his hand between her legs and explored her swollen center.

It took him less than three seconds to find that one magical spot. He circled it before settling down to a perfect, rhythmic caress that made the end inevitable.

She sank into the sensation, letting her body take over. Tension built until she could barely breathe. Her fingers curled into the blanket, her heels dug into the mattress. Todd shifted so he could claim her mouth and when his tongue touched hers, she lost herself in blissful release.

Her climax seemed to go on forever. Wave after wave of perfection rocked through her, sucking away her will to do anything but feel this forever.

Eventually, though, she became aware of his hardness pressing into her leg. She opened her eyes and found Todd smiling down at her.

"That was good," he said. "At least it was good for me. I'm thinking it was better than good for you."

"It was," she said as she traced his lower lip with her thumb. "Ready for some better than good of your own?"

"I thought you'd never ask."

He eased between her thighs, then pushed until she felt him entering her. He was big and thick, stretching her. She arched her hips toward him, wanting to take all of him. He withdrew, entered her again and she wrapped her arms round him, pulling him against her, enjoying the weight of him nearly as much as what he was doing to her body.

Because it had begun again. The sense of need and wanting. The growing heat as muscles tightened in anticipation of a spectacular ride. Faster and faster, pushing, filling. Her breathing became as ragged as his. She felt his arms begin to tremble as he sought that moment of no return.

She'd been empty for so long that she'd forgotten the glory of being filled by a man intent on pleasing them both.

He bent down and kissed her as the sensations claimed her, and then he groaned and pushed in deeper. She felt him stiffen before he stilled and shuddered.

When they'd cleaned up and slid under the covers, Julie rested her head on his shoulder. He had his arm around her, she had her thigh nestled against his. This was one of life's perfect moments, she thought happily. Those times she would look back on later and think, *That was a great night.*

"Thank you," he said as he played with her hair. "That was pretty…"

"Spectacular?" she asked, feeling content.

"I was going to say *amazing*, but *spectacular* works."

She closed her eyes and smiled. "I'm deeply out of practice. I appreciate the lesson bringing me up to speed."

"You didn't act like you were out of practice. You acted like you'd read the manual on how to push all my buttons."

The smile turned into a grin. "Really? All of them?"

"Well, maybe you missed one."

"I'll have to catch that next time."

He chuckled. "Words to make a man your love slave forever. Can I stay?"

Three little words that got her attention in a big way. She might have been out of the dating game for a while, but she remembered most of the rules. After sex, especially an encounter so unexpected, most guys preferred to dress and run. She didn't have a lot of personal experience, but she'd had enough friends cry on her shoulder to be familiar with the practice.

Todd wanted to stay? Here? With her? Tonight?

A little bubble of happiness floated up from her tummy to her chest where it gave birth to about a thousand other little bubbles.

"I had plans for later," she said, deciding going for casual was best for both of them. "I guess I can cancel them."

"I appreciate that. Do you snore?"

She laughed. "No, do you?"

"I'm a very quiet sleeper." He shifted so that he could kiss her. "Not that I expect either of us to get much sleep tonight."

Sometime after two in the morning, he watched the moonlight on Julie's face and knew he'd made a mess of things from the beginning.

It wasn't supposed to have been like this. He wasn't supposed to like her. From what he'd been told, Julie Nelson was a gold-digging bimbo who needed a good lesson and he'd been just the man to volunteer to teach it. He'd expected a vapid, over-accessorized bitch.

Instead he'd found a beautiful, funny, intelligent, sincere woman who made him laugh and want to believe in possibilities again.

Right now he should be feeling as if he'd done the world a favor. Instead he felt like a total jerk. He'd just created a hell of a mess and he had no idea how to fix it. He liked Julie. He liked her a lot.

How was he supposed to explain that he wasn't Todd Aston III, and that she'd just been set up to take a fall?

Three

Julie stood in her kitchen and held on to the edge of the counter. It wasn't that the world was spinning so much as she thought it might at any moment. She half expected a bolt of lightning to come crashing through the roof, or at the very least, hear the ghost of Christmas Past.

There was a man in her bedroom.

Right now, even while she was supposed to be making coffee, Todd lay asleep in her bed.

Until he had stepped inside last night, her place had been a man-free zone. After what had happened with Garrett, she'd wanted to keep it that way. She'd rented it after law school, furnished it with girlie stuff and her mattress had been practically virginal.

Not anymore, she thought with a grin as she reached

for the can of coffee and the scooper next to it. She had languid, morning-after glow and a couple of sore muscles to prove it.

She added water and flipped on the coffeemaker, then leaned against the counter. In theory she should probably be having regrets or even second thoughts. Last night really wasn't like her at all. She was more sensible, more careful, much less impetuous. Which she would go back to being very soon. Right now she just wanted to wallow in the hot memories of what they'd done.

She felt good—too good to feel bad.

"Morning."

She glanced up and saw Todd standing in the doorway to the kitchen. He'd pulled on his slacks and his shirt, but hadn't buttoned the latter. She could see bare skin and tapered muscles. He also looked mussed, unshaven and too sexy for words.

Unexpected shyness gripped her. "Hi," she murmured, then cleared her throat. "I'm making coffee, which you can probably guess."

"Good. Thanks."

His dark gaze settled on her face. She had to fight the need to smooth her hair, even though before entering the kitchen she'd stopped in the bathroom to wash her face, brush her teeth and make sure her hair didn't look as if it had been attacked by angry birds.

She had no idea what he was thinking. He probably did this sort of thing most mornings, woke up in a strange bed. She could let him set the tone. Except that wasn't her style. She was far more take-charge. Her sisters would be happy to provide testimony on her behalf.

"So I'm out of practice," she said with a shrug. "The whole strange-guy-in-my-bed and all that. I didn't expect last night so I certainly didn't prepare for this morning. What would you like to do? Shower? Leave? Get my phone number?"

He folded his arms over his chest and leaned against the door frame. "You're honest."

"As I was last night. It's kind of something that sticks with me. I like to think I'm a trendsetter. Plus, I've never understood the thrill of lying. The truth comes out eventually."

"Interesting point. What are your plans for the day?"

Plans? It *was* a Saturday. "I, ah, have to run some errands. I brought some work home and I'm meeting my sisters later for lunch."

"Busy lady."

"It happens. And you? What are you doing today?"

"Meeting my cousin, but that's not until later." He glanced down the hall, then back at her. "Can I take you up on that shower? Maybe borrow a toothbrush?"

"Sure."

This was so weird, she thought as she moved down the hall and opened the small linen closet by the bathroom. There was a single unwrapped toothbrush, which was, unfortunately, bright pink.

"Sorry," she murmured.

"I'll survive. Do your razors have flowers on them?"

"No, but they're mostly purple."

"Such a girl."

"Would you be more comfortable if I were a guy?" she asked.

He shuddered. "No. Although it would have made for an interesting conversation."

She handed him a couple of towels, then pointed to the bathroom. "Have at it."

"Okay, thanks."

She returned to the kitchen and reached for a mug. There was a man in her bathroom. A soon-to-be naked man who would shower and use her soap and it was all very strange. She should—

"Julie?"

She set down the mug and walked back into the hall. The bathroom door stood partially open.

"What? Is there a problem?" she asked.

"Sort of."

She paused just outside the bathroom and opened her mouth to speak. But before she could say anything, he grabbed her arm and pulled her inside.

He was naked. She grasped that much right before he drew her close and kissed her. Naked and hard and apparently still in the mood, she thought happily as she parted her lips and let the games begin. His tongue teased hers before he shifted his attention to her neck.

"You're wearing a robe," he murmured against her skin.

"Yes, I am." She sounded breathless, which made sense. She *was* breathless.

"That's gotta go."

He was a man of his word. He tugged the tie loose, then pushed the robe off her body. She was naked underneath—a good thing what with the way he immediately began to caress her breasts.

His touch was inspired, she thought as her mind began to fog as passion and need took over. In a matter of seconds she was wet and swollen and hungry for him to be inside of her.

While he bent down and licked her tight, sensitive nipples, she rubbed his shoulders, his back, then kissed the top of his head.

He straightened. "Okay, time to shower."

Shower? "What?"

He took her hand and guided her into the tub, then pulled the curtain closed. He urged her under the spray, then reached for the soap.

After lathering his hands, he began to wash her all over. The soap made her skin slick. His fingers glided and slipped as he first cleaned her, then teased her.

He washed her back, her hips, the backs of her legs, before rinsing her off. Then instead of turning her, he just moved in close and with her back pressing against his chest, began to run his hands up and down the front of her body.

He caressed her neck, then did a thorough job of cleaning her breasts. The combination of soapy fingers against her nipples and pounding hot water made her weak and hungry with need. She covered his hands with hers to keep him in place while she leaned her head against his shoulder.

"There's more," he whispered in her ear. "Much more."

Without warning, he stepped back, then turned her. He lightly kissed her on the mouth before dropping to his knees and pressing another opened-mouthed kiss to her stomach.

Her muscles clenched in anticipation. The water ran down her body. He urged her to put one foot on the edge of the tub, then he leaned in, parted her flesh and licked her. She cried out as his tongue circled the very heart of her, before moving across her swollen center. She felt his lips, his breath and the steady pressure as he pleasured her.

She had to brace herself by placing one hand on the wall. Her legs began to tremble as her muscles clenched. He moved slow, then fast, licking, sucking, forcing her higher and closer. Her breath came in pants. She was completely his to command as the promise of an incredible orgasm kept her frozen in place.

She wanted to beg. If she'd known any state secrets she would have yelled them, anything to have him keep doing what he was doing. She felt herself spiral closer and yet her release remained elusively out of reach.

More, she thought frantically, she needed more. But how?

He must have read her mind because he slipped two fingers inside of her. Even as he continued to kiss her so intimately, he filled her and the combination was too much.

She lost control right there, in the shower, with the water pounding and an incredible man between her legs. She gasped for breath and screamed and shuddered until she knew that nothing ever again would ever be this spectacular.

Her release crashed through her, leaving her exhausted and boneless. Todd stood and smiled, then pulled her close. She could barely gather the strength to hug him back.

The thought of doing to him what he'd gone to her perked her up a little. She stepped back, but before she could do anything else, he reached behind her and turned off the shower.

"We'll get cold," she told him.

"I don't think so."

He pulled open the curtains, then led her out of the shower. After spreading a towel on the counter, he lifted her onto it, parted her legs and pushed into her with one firm, demanding thrust.

She would have bet a lot of money that she was too content to even think about coming again for six or eight months. But the second he filled her, she felt tired muscles sit up and take notice. Then he kissed her and she found herself getting lost in the sensual dance of tongues and lips and need.

They were both wet and the bathroom was steamy and he hadn't had a real shower yet, but none of that mattered. Not when he slipped his hand between them and found her still-swollen center. He rubbed it gently enough not to hurt, but just enough to make her surge toward him.

She went from exhausted to take-me-now in less than fifteen seconds. She wrapped her legs around his hips and rode him until she came again—this time holding in her scream until he groaned her name and they got lost together in their mutual release.

Julie lay on her bed, her eyes closed, her long, blond hair spread out on the pillow. Ryan Bennett twisted a strand around his index finger, enjoying the softness of her hair and the way it caught the light. Her breathing was slow and steady, as if she were about to fall sleep, but the slight smile tugging at the corners of her mouth told him she might have something else on her mind.

Something he would find very appealing.

He didn't want to go. That surprised him nearly as much as anything. Normally he was a get-out-of-town-fast kind of guy, the morning after. He frequently avoided the problem by not staying at all. But he'd wanted to wake up in Julie's bed and make love with her again. He'd wanted a lot of things.

"Julie," he murmured.

She opened her eyes. Her irises were a blue with tiny flecks of green. She had freckles and a wicked smile, and she smelled like vanilla and sex and temptation.

How could she be like that and be a scheming liar? Was this all a game to her? A twisted, win-at-any-cost game?

He'd pretended not to know about Ruth's offer of a million dollars to see if she would mention it. She had, though, and in such a way that he wanted to believe it didn't matter to her. But if she didn't care about the money, why go on the date at all?

She reached up and stroked his face. "You're far too good-looking," she told him.

"That's not a bad thing."

"It could be. Handsome men don't have to try so hard."

"So you'd rather I was a troll?"

"I'd like to think you had to put a little effort into getting women into your bed. Instead, I have a feeling I'm simply one of the masses."

"I didn't get you into my bed," he said as he leaned close. "I got you into your bed."

"That's a subtlety that does nothing to weaken my point."

He rolled onto his side and supported his head with his hand. "Why do you get away with saying bad things about men, but if I were to make a crack about beautiful women, you'd accuse me of being misogynistic?"

"Because it would be true. We have centuries of inequity between the sexes to overcome. I think a little head start for the ladies is perfectly acceptable."

"So speaks the lady."

She raised her eyebrows. "We've already had the 'do you want me to be a man' conversation. Yet here we are, flirting with it again. Is there something you want to tell me?"

He rolled onto his back. "You're driving me crazy."

"It's one of my best qualities. I've turned it into an art form."

She laughed, then bent over him and brushed his mouth with hers. Her hair stroked his chest and it was all he could do not to reach out and touch her, take her, be inside of her.

Who was she, really? He'd come on the date because Todd was his cousin and he, Ryan, had been in the mood to exact a little revenge on money-hungry women, whomever they might be. He hadn't cared about Julie; in fact, he'd been prepared to dislike her on sight.

But she'd won him over and somehow made him want to believe in her.

"Tell me about your family," he said.

She raised her head. "Interesting change in topic."

"I'm curious about your grandmother. How could you not know her all these years?"

Julie curled up next to him and put her head on his shoulder. Involuntarily, he reached for her hand and laced their fingers together.

"Ruth's first husband died unexpectedly, while she was pregnant with my mom. Ruth remarried a few months after the birth to Fraser Jamison, your great-uncle. Naomi, my mom, looked on him as her father. When she was seventeen, she met Jack Nelson, my dad, and fell madly in love with him. He didn't come from money—in fact he was a bit of a loser, but charming and she couldn't help herself. She ran off and married him, and Ruth and Fraser turned their backs on her."

The story matched what Ryan had been told, although his uncle Fraser hadn't been that generous in the telling. He'd painted Naomi as an ungrateful slut who'd defied him at every turn and her husband as a money-grabbing bastard who'd been out for what he could get.

"My mom was pregnant, of course. I was born six months after the wedding. My two sisters followed very quickly. Mom got a job, Dad tried, but he wasn't the type to enjoy real work. Although he always had a scam going. Some of them even paid off. He took off for the first time when I was about eight. He'd be gone for months at a time, then show up. He'd bring us gifts and her money, then he'd leave again."

There was anger in her voice, and maybe a little pain. Was either emotion real? "That must have been hard for you," he said.

She sighed. "I wanted her to divorce him and move

on, but she wouldn't. She said he was the love of her life. I thought he was a jerk who couldn't stand to take responsibility for his family. But that's a fascinating discussion for another time. Years passed, we all grew up. Then about three months ago, Ruth appeared on our doorstep. She said that she'd been wanting to reconcile with her daughter for a long time, but Fraser had stood in the way. With him gone, she was free to do as she wanted and have her family back. So now we have a grandmother."

And a potential inheritance, he thought cynically. "She came to you?"

"That's what I heard. Mom called and asked us all to join her for dinner. We walked in and there was Ruth." She raised her head and looked at him. "It's weird to suddenly find out about relatives this long after the fact."

That he could agree with. "What do you think about her?"

"She's crusty," Julie said as she wrinkled her nose. "Very elegant, but distant and…I don't know. I don't really know her. I guess I'm mad because she turned her only daughter away. Okay, sure, she didn't approve of what my mom did, but there's a whole lot of space between not approving and never seeing her again. She turned her back on all of us. Now she says she's sorry and we're supposed to just forgive her? Pretend all those years without her didn't matter?"

He found himself in the odd position of wanting to defend his aunt. Ironic, considering he, too, thought of her as meddling and difficult. Still, he loved her.

"She's getting older," he said. "Maybe losing her husband has caused her to see what's really important."

She looked at him. "Do *not* tell me you're a middle child?"

"I'm an only child."

"You don't sound like it. Willow is the middle sister and she's forever seeing everyone else's point of view. It's an incredibly annoying characteristic."

"In my business it's important to see all sides of a situation."

"I'm not sure that's a good enough excuse."

He wanted to believe her. He hadn't expected that, but then he hadn't expected a lot of things.

"I'm not trying to jump to conclusions here," she said, "but you do realize that despite all this, we can't get involved."

Couldn't they? "Why not?"

"Because of my crazy grandmother and your crazy aunt."

"We're not related."

"It's the money. If we got involved, everyone would think it was because of the tantalizing offer of a million dollars. *You* would think that. I don't get it. You are not the kind of man who needs anyone's help to get a woman. So why would she do that?"

"Ruth has some particular ideas about life and her place in everyone else's." She always had. Maybe she genuinely thought one of her granddaughters would be able to trap Todd. Ryan was more willing to bet on his cousin. Todd wasn't interested in anything serious and no one was going to change his mind.

"Like I said. Crazy." Julie shrugged. "But now we have a problem."

Everything about her screamed that she was telling the truth. She met his gaze easily, she wasn't nervous. She'd been funny and charming and blunt ever since she'd walked up to his table in the restaurant and had compared him to Mr. Howell.

"You're saying things would be better if I was an impoverished shoe salesman?" he asked.

"In a way. Although it sounds a little nineteenth century. Couldn't you just be a high-school math teacher or an entry-level computer programmer?"

"I could be, but I'm not."

"So now what?" She reached for her robe and pulled it on, then sat up and smiled at him. "I'm presuming you want to see me again, mostly because I've given you many opportunities to bolt for freedom and you haven't taken any of them."

"Do you wish I would have?"

"No." She shrugged again. "I kind of like having you around." She laughed. "This time yesterday I was dreading meeting you. I wished that either of my sisters could have been paid to take my place. But now..." She touched his hand. "Sometimes losing is a good thing."

His chest tightened as the truth slammed into him. Whatever he and Todd had thought about Julie Nelson, they'd been wrong. She wasn't in this for the money. She wasn't in it for any reason other than she'd wanted to make her grandmother happy and she'd lost a stupid game.

The realization of what he'd done—how he'd blown it—made him sick. He'd thought she'd be a bitch—

instead she was the most amazing woman he'd ever met, and he'd screwed this up. Totally.

"Todd?" she asked. "What's wrong? You have the strangest look on your face."

"I…" He swore silently. How to explain? How to… "I'm not Todd Aston."

Four

Julie knew she was supposed to say something, but she couldn't seem to get her brain to work. Too little sleep and too much shock made thinking impossible.

"You're not Todd?" she asked, more to herself than him.

"Julie, look," he began, but she raised her hand to cut him off.

"You're not Todd," she repeated as she stared at the naked man in her bed. The man she'd made love with several times. The man she'd laughed with and joked with and had taken her clothes off for and *trusted*?

"You're not Todd?"

This time the words came out in a yell that gave voice to the fury and horror building inside of her. She scrambled off the bed and tightened the belt of her robe.

"What the hell do you mean, you're not Todd?"

"I'm his cousin, Ryan Bennett. Todd and I knew about what Ruth had done, and we figured anyone who agreed to her terms was only in it for the money. I went on this date thinking I was here to teach you a lesson. You know, pretend to be Todd and then cut out."

"His *cousin*? This was just a game to you? Is this your idea of a good time?" She glared at him and wished she worked out so she could punch him and have it hurt.

Todd or Ryan or whatever his name was climbed out of bed and stood in front of her. Naked. Gorgeous. But that shouldn't be a surprise. Why wouldn't evil, lying, snake bastards be good-looking, too?

"Julie, wait. It's not what you think."

"Don't even try," she told him, feeling light-headed from the rage coursing through her. "Don't think you can smooth talk your way out of this one."

"I don't want to talk myself out of anything—I want to explain. I didn't mean for this to happen."

This? As in the sex? The rage built and she was suddenly terrified she was going to cry. Oh, God, not that. She refused to break down in front of this weasel.

"What part didn't you mean?" she asked, her voice thick with loathing. "The part where we agreed to meet for dinner? Or was it just a slip of the tongue when you introduced yourself as Todd? Oops, silly me. I forgot my name?"

He'd been charming, she thought, just as enraged at herself as she was at him. Of course—if *she'd* fallen for him, there had to be something wrong with him. It wasn't as if she ever found someone decent. He'd been funny and smart and she'd been so attracted to him. Hadn't that been enough of a warning in her brain? But no. She had to go and think he was what he seemed. She had to go and bring him home and have sex with him.

For someone who was supposed to be so damn bright, why did she have to act so stupid?

"We thought…" he began.

"You thought what? This would be good sport? No, wait. What was it you said? You were going to teach me a lesson?" She glanced at her lamp and thought about flinging it at his head. "Who the hell are you to be judge and jury? What did I ever do to you?"

"You didn't do anything," he told her earnestly. "Nothing at all. You're the innocent party in this. I'm sorry."

"Sorry doesn't cut it."

"I know. When Aunt Ruth told Todd what she'd done, what she'd promised you and your sisters, he was furious. He always has money-hungry women chasing after him and he didn't need three more trying to marry him for his wealth."

"Todd needs to get over himself," she said bitterly. "It wasn't about the money. You know that, damn you. It was about finding out we had a grandmother and keeping things good between us. No one thought her offer was real. What's wrong with you people?"

"You have no idea what it's like," he said.

"Oh, poor little rich boy. I bleed for your pain."

He was still naked and she deeply resented that part of her brain could actually pause and appreciate the sculpted perfection of his body. Her insides quivered at the memory of being taken by him over and over again.

She sucked in a breath and pointed at the door. "Get out. Get out now."

"Julie, you have to understand. I never thought I'd be meeting *you*."

There were a thousand ways to interpret that sentence. She had a feeling it was his meager attempt to tell her that she was special, that she mattered.

Oh, please. "So if you hadn't liked me, it would have been okay to screw with me? There's a nice statement about your character."

He flinched slightly. "I didn't mean it like that."

"Sure you did. You're not sorry you tried to teach me a lesson, because even knowing nothing about me, you were confident I deserved one. No, your only problem comes from the fact that I was someone you enjoyed being with and now you've screwed things so totally I wouldn't get involved with you if you were the last man on the planet. There is nothing you can say or do to ever convince me you are anything but a lying bastard who believes he is so superior to everyone around him that he gets to cast judgment on the rest of the world. You are self-centered, egotistical, rude and twisted in ways I can't begin to comprehend. Now get the hell out of my house."

He drew in a breath, then nodded. After gathering his clothes, he walked out of the bedroom. Less than a minute later, the front door opened and he was gone.

Julie sank onto the floor. At least he was a fast

dresser, she thought as waves of pain washed over her. And he was gone.

She began to shake as she fought tears and she hated that through all of this, she'd desperately wanted him to beg. She knew it couldn't have made any difference, but she'd wanted it all the same. She'd wanted to know that last night had meant as much to him as it had to her.

Obviously, it hadn't.

Julie dressed in her tightest pair of jeans because being unable to breathe helped to keep her mind off the horrors of her morning. She'd scrubbed the shower, washed her sheets, remade the bed and had given herself a stern talking-to. None of that had worked in the least, so she'd left to go see her sisters, stopping on the way to buy the biggest latte known to man. If not breathing didn't help, maybe she could drown herself from the inside out.

It was a little after eleven when she pulled up in front of the small house where she'd grown up. The tiny lawn looked lush and green and there were flowering plants everywhere, mostly thanks to Willow's green thumb.

She glanced at the two cars already parked in front of the house and took in the empty space in the driveway, then got out and walked into the house.

"Hey, it's me," she said as she stepped into the bright living room.

Willow sat curled up in the chair in the corner, while Marina had taken a corner of the sofa. They both smiled at her.

"Hi," Willow said as she stood and hugged her sister. "Are you really going to drink all that coffee? Too much of that will kill you."

"That's the plan," Julie said, doing her best to smile as she spoke so Willow would think she was kidding.

Marina moved in for her hug. "Hi. How are things?"

"Okay. Mom at the clinic?"

"Uh-huh." Marina sat back on the sofa and patted the cushion next to her. "It's low-cost vaccination day."

"Right." Julie plopped down.

One Saturday morning a month, Dr. Greenberg, Naomi's boss, opened his offices to the neighborhood and gave low-cost vaccinations to whomever wanted them. It had been their mother's idea—part of her ongoing quest to save the world. Julie had always thought she should spend a little more time trying to save herself.

"So how are you two?" she asked.

Willow and Marina exchanged a glance. Julie immediately tensed. "What?"

Willow sighed. "We were talking about Dad."

Great. Because the day hadn't started off badly enough, Julie thought grimly.

"It's been a few months," Marina said. "He should be coming back any time now."

"How exciting," Julie muttered and sipped more coffee.

"Jules, no." Willow flipped her long blond hair off her shoulder and leaned forward. "That's not fair. You never give him a break."

"I'm sorry I don't have enough appreciation for a man who abandons his family over and over again and the mother who lets him."

Marina's mouth twisted. "That's not fair. She loves him."

Julie felt too raw to deal with the familiar argument. "Don't say he's her destiny, I beg you. He blows back into her life and ours, he's charming and adoring and then he goes away. He moves on to the next thrill and we're left picking up the pieces."

Julie's childhood had been punctuated by her father's visits and her mother's subsequent week of tears and feeble attempts to hide her pain. While her sisters were happy to remember the excitement of their father's visit, Julie always recalled the aftermath. Jack Nelson was like a big electrical storm. A lot of light and noise and an impressive show, but when it was over, someone had to handle the cleanup. That someone had usually been her.

She took another sip of her coffee. Apparently it wasn't enough to drown her, which meant she would now be completely awake to deal with the humiliation of last night and this morning.

"All men are bastards," she muttered.

Willow's blue eyes widened. "Julie, no. Not all guys are like Garrett."

Right. Her ex-fiancé. Julie groaned. She'd thought he'd been the absolute low point of her romantic life, but when compared with Todd/Ryan, he was almost a nice guy.

"Speaking of slime on two legs," she said, "I had my date with Todd last night."

"What?" Marina threw a pillow at Julie. "Are you kidding? Why didn't you say anything until now?"

"I've been here five minutes."

Willow rolled her eyes. "Oh, please. That's a walk-in announcement and you know it." She slid to the edge of the chair and grinned. "Okay, tell us everything. Start at the beginning and speak slowly. Don't leave out anything. Was he fabulous? Was he charming? Could you tell he was rich?"

Under any other circumstances, Julie would have laughed. Willow's idea of a guy with money was one who would only make her pay for her own meal instead of his as well. She tended to attract the down-and-out type, those between jobs or paychecks or even stints in jail.

"He was…"

On the way over, Julie had tried to come up with a way to make the situation into something she could laugh about instead of a pathetic statement on her luck with men. But she couldn't remember a single thing she'd planned on saying and she surprised both herself and most likely her sisters by starting to cry.

"Jules?"

They were both beside her in a heartbeat. Marina hugged her from the side and Willow knelt in front of her. Someone took her coffee from her hand, and then she was held so hard, her chest hurt. Or maybe her chest just hurt on its own.

The embrace was familiar and comforting. They'd always been there for each other, only she wasn't usually the one at the center of the healing.

Julie wiped away her tears and swallowed. "He wasn't a one-armed humpback," she said, her voice shaking a little. "He was nice. Charming and sexy and we danced and he made me laugh."

She'd already decided not to mention that she'd slept with him. No doubt she would confess all later, but right now she couldn't face admitting she'd been that much of a fool.

She'd been so careful, too. Ever since Garrett, she'd avoided men and sex and entanglements. Based on who Ryan had turned out to be, she should have stuck with being single.

"How did it go wrong?" Willow asked. "Was he secretly a woman?"

That made Julie laugh. She touched her sister's face. "No, but that would have been interesting. He lied...about everything."

She told them about him pretending to be Todd, in order to teach her a lesson.

"He assumed I was in it for the money, so his plan was to show me a good time, get me to fall for him and then tell me the truth."

"What?" Marina stood up and put her hands on his hips. "That's horrible. You didn't do it for the money. You did it for Grandma Ruth. You lost. Did you tell him you lost because you always play scissors?"

"I mentioned that."

Marina settled back beside her. "This is going to turn you off guys forever, isn't it?"

Julie nodded. "I suspect I'll have a lengthy recovery."

"Want me to hurt him for you?" Willow asked.

Julie laughed again. Willow was all of five foot three inches. She was feisty on the inside but on the outside she had a whole lot more in common with a waif than a bodybuilder.

"That's okay," Julie told her. "I appreciate the offer, but he's big and burly."

"But I have speed and the element of surprise on my side."

"I love you guys," Julie said.

"We love you, too," Marina told her. "I'm just so mad. Maybe Willow and I could take him together."

"I don't think so."

Willow leaned against Julie's shoulder. "I hate Todd, too. He's a part of this. How could Grandma Ruth want any of us to marry someone who's so jerky?"

"Maybe she doesn't know," Marina murmured.

"Maybe it's the reason she offered the money," Julie said. "It doesn't matter. It's over. I'm never going to see Ryan again."

Or think of him. Except she had a feeling that forgetting him was going to be more difficult than she wanted it to be. If only she could go back in time and never show up for that stupid date.

Willow squeezed her arm. "You want us to not tell Mom? You know how she worries."

"That would be great," Julie said. "I'll probably have to mention it eventually, but if I could wait a while, it would be easier."

"Sure," Marina said. "Whatever you want."

Julie managed a smile. "So you two feel so sorry for me I could get you to do anything, huh?"

Her sisters nodded.

If she'd been feeling better, she might have teased them or come up with a crazy task. Instead she let them comfort her and told herself that in time, she would put all this behind her and forget she'd ever known Ryan Bennett.

Julie stared out of the window of her office and did her best to get excited about the view. Sure, she could mostly see the building next door, but to the right she could see clear to Long Beach.

She'd been promoted the previous week and had moved into larger quarters. She now had a shared assistant and a nice raise. She also had big plans to celebrate this weekend with a shopping spree. Willow and Marina had already promised to come with her.

This was all good. She was smart, successful, moving upward in her chosen career. So why couldn't she stop thinking about Ryan?

It had been three weeks since that disastrous night and morning when he'd swept into her life and made her think this time things would be different. Three weeks of remembering, of dreaming about him, of wanting him.

That's what she resented most—that her own body betrayed her. She could stay sane during the day but when she finally fell asleep, he invaded her dreams as she relived what it had been like to be with him. She woke up several times a night, aroused, hungry for his touch. These were not the signs of a woman forgetting a man.

"I want him gone," she whispered into the silence.

But how to make that happen? Until she'd found out he was a lying bastard, he'd been the best night of her life.

He was also persistent. He'd phoned three times and

sent a basket filled with chocolate, wine and season one of *Gilligan's Island* on DVD.

She placed her hand on the cool glass. Things had to get better, right? She couldn't remember him forever. It was a matter of discipline and maybe a little less coffee. She could always call Willow—the queen of all things organic—and ask if there was some kind of sleep aid to get her through this rough patch.

Julie turned to return to her desk, only she didn't exactly make it. As she took a step, the room seemed to shift and sway.

Her first thought was an earthquake, but there wasn't any noise. Her second thought was that she'd never felt so dizzy in her life. Her vision narrowed and she realized she was very possibly going to faint.

Somehow she made it to her chair where she collapsed. After a couple of deep breaths, her head cleared, but now her stomach felt all queasy.

She did a quick review of what she'd eaten that day and wondered if she had food poisoning. When that seemed unlikely, she considered a quick-onset flu. It was early in the season, but it could happen.

Wasn't there a prescription she could take? Something that would cut down how long she would be sick. Eyeing the stack of work awaiting her attention, she picked up the phone and dialed a familiar number.

"Hi, Mom, it's me. I'm good. Kind of. Is there a flu going around?"

"How do you feel?" her mother asked two hours later as Julie sat in one of Dr. Greenberg's examining rooms. One of the advantages of her mother being the man's office manager was Julie and her sisters never had to wait to get an appointment.

She'd been weighed, had her blood pressure taken, peed in a cup. Talk about thorough. "I feel weird," Julie admitted. "Queasy, but otherwise fine. I keep waiting to throw up, but I don't."

"Poor girl," Naomi said soothingly as she held her hand against her daughter's forehead.

"I'm twenty-six, Mom. Not really girl material."

Her mother smiled. "You'll always be my little girl."

Julie laughed. Right now the fussing was kind of nice.

"Let me get you something carbonated," her mother said as she headed for the door. "It might settle your stomach."

Julie watched her go. All three sisters had inherited their mother's blond hair and blue eyes. They were variations on a theme, ranging from Willow's pale blond to Julie's medium, to Marina's dark gold hair. Julie and Marina had inherited their father's height, while Willow was petite.

In her high-school science class, Julie had been fascinated by how two people could have produced three daughters who were so similar in some ways and different in others.

"Here you go." Her mother returned with an iced drink in a cartoon-character paper cup. "Dr. Greenberg will be right in."

Just then the older man stepped into the room. "Julie, you never come see me anymore. What's up with that?

Now that you're a fancy lawyer, you don't have any time for a mere doctor?"

"I do move in very special circles," she said with a grin.

Her mother waved and ducked out of the room. Dr. Greenberg took Julie's hand and leaned forward to kiss her on her cheek.

"So you're not feeling too good?" he asked.

"I don't know. It's weird. I can't tell if it's food poisoning or the flu. I thought maybe you could tell me and then give me a prescription."

He scowled at her, an expression she remembered from when she'd been little and had been scratching her rampant case of poison ivy.

"Not everything can be solved with a pill, young lady."

She fingered the long sleeve of her silk blouse. "Does this make me look too young? First Mom and now you. Do I look sixteen?"

"I'm lecturing you," he said. "You could listen and pretend to be intimidated."

"Oh. Sorry."

He shook his head and settled on the stool. "You girls."

She smiled.

Dr. Greenberg had been a part of their lives for as long as Julie could remember. He was a warm, caring widower. When she'd finally figured out her father would always show up only to leave again, she'd started hoping her mother would divorce him and marry Dr. Greenberg.

"All right." He flipped through her chart. "You're basically healthy. Good blood pressure. You getting enough sleep?"

She thought about the Ryan dreams. "Too much."

"Like I believe that. You work too hard, but you can slow down a little. The firm will survive."

"Slow down? Why? What's wrong with me? Is it more serious than the flu?"

He set down her chart and looked at her. "You're going to have to be the one to decide that. You're not sick, Julie. You're pregnant."

Five

"They have a unique take on the market," Todd said from his seat across the conference table. "This would be a new area for us. We've talked about expanding and—"

Todd broke off and tossed down the folder. "Am I boring you?"

Ryan glanced at his cousin, then at the paperwork in front of him. "It sounds like a great opportunity."

Todd glowered at him. "You could at least pretend to care about the damn business. What's wrong with you? It's not that Nelson woman again? It can't be. It's been too long."

Not for him, Ryan thought, feeling both angry with himself and resigned to the situation. His attempts to contact Julie had gotten him nowhere. He'd blown it and he had to accept that. The thing was, he didn't want to.

Todd leaned toward him. "Dammit, Ryan, what's the big deal? Women have been after us since we were fifteen years old. The money is just too hard to resist. We're both sick of being the catch of the day. So why now? Why this woman?"

"An excellent question," Ryan admitted. "I don't have an answer except to say she was amazing and I destroyed any chance I had with her."

"So you pretended to be me," Todd said. "What's the big deal? If she's all that, then why can't she see the humor in the situation?"

Ryan didn't answer. He'd given Todd a very abbreviated version of his date with Julie, leaving out the fact that he'd spent the night.

"I swear, Aunt Ruth can be a pain," Todd muttered. "When she suggested I marry one of her granddaughters, I wanted to choke her."

"I wanted to help," Ryan said, knowing he'd gone into the situation willingly. The idea of exacting a little revenge had been too appealing to ignore.

He'd let his pride take charge, always a dangerous decision.

"Julie didn't do anything wrong," he said, more to himself than Todd, "and I hurt her."

"She was willing to go out with a man for money," Todd pointed out. "That's something."

Despite feeling like roadkill, Ryan smiled. "The date was free. I told her she should have held out for at least fifty thousand. After all, there had to be something significantly wrong with you for your own aunt to have to pay someone to marry you."

Predictably, Todd bristled. "She's my aunt by marriage and there's nothing wrong with me."

He and Todd were enough alike that Ryan had to agree. Despite only being cousins, they were so similar in appearance that they had often been asked if they were twins. But for once, he and Todd were going to part company. On the issue of Julie Nelson, Ryan could only have regrets.

"You're going to have to forget her," Todd said.

"I will." In time. The question was, how long would it take?

"Look at the bright side. If this went as badly as you said, I don't have to worry about the other Nelson sisters wanting to marry me. So you've derailed Aunt Ruth."

"She'll come up with another plan. You know she wants to see us both married. You got picked first because you're a whole couple of months older, but my time is coming."

He had the sudden thought that if he *had* been picked first, then his date with Julie would have been real. He would have gone, expecting nothing, determined to get rid of Julie as quickly as possible, and she still would have won him over.

He felt both sad and angry at the thought. Yes, he'd screwed up. He was willing to admit that, even crawl a little. Why was she so stubborn? Was the situation really that unrecoverable?

He already knew the answer and, as he only had himself to blame, he had nowhere to put the excess emotion.

"I'm going to the gym," he said as he stood. Maybe

a couple of hours on the running track or in the weight room would allow him to sleep tonight. Or at the very least, forget for a few minutes.

But before he could leave, the door to the conference room opened and his secretary stepped in.

"Sorry to interrupt, but there's someone here to see Ryan. A Julie Nelson. She says it's important. Should I show her in?"

Todd looked at Ryan. "She must have checked out your latest financials and realized it's a hell of a lot of money."

"Shut up," Ryan said without looking at him. "Yes, Mandy, please show her in."

Seconds later Julie walked into the room. His chest tightened and he felt as stupid and clueless as a high-school sophomore on his first date. Relief, desire and excitement battled for his attention.

She was gorgeous—tall and blond with blue eyes that flashed her every emotion. Right now they held a combination of controlled rage and contempt.

"Good morning," she said, her voice as low and sexy as it had been every night in his dreams. The navy power suit she wore concealed more than it showed, but he remembered the curves and soft skin underneath. Dear God, he remembered.

She glanced from him to Todd, then smiled coldly.

"There's enough similarity in your appearance for me to know who you are," she said. "The infamous Todd Aston III. It's my lucky day. Two snakes for the price of one. The liar and the man afraid to do his own dirty work. Your mothers must be so proud."

Todd raised his eyebrows and nodded slightly. Ryan knew his cousin well enough to read his thoughts. Todd was impressed that Julie wasn't stupid and wasn't begging. If Julie had known that, she would have probably told Todd he needed to date a wider range of women.

Ryan liked that he could predict what she was going to say—only the talent wouldn't have much use. From the looks of things, she hadn't dropped in to forgive him.

"I didn't expect to see you again," Ryan told her.

"It's all about net worth," Todd said, staring at Julie. "Isn't it?"

"I'd wondered why your aunt felt it necessary to offer money to get someone to marry you," Julie said calmly. "I'd thought the reason might have something to do with a physical impairment. Now I realize the flaw is in your personality. How unfortunate and much more difficult to fix." She looked at Ryan. "I need to speak with you privately. Now is a good time for me."

Todd stood, then raised both his hands in the air. "I'll leave," he said to Ryan. "Later you can try to explain what exactly it was that you missed."

With that he left. Ryan pointed at the empty chairs around the table. "Have a seat."

She hesitated, then sat down. He could feel the anger radiating from her.

"I called," he said, knowing it was pointless, but still compelled to make the effort.

"I got the messages."

"And the basket?"

"That's not why I'm here."

"You never said thank you."

Her eyes widened in outrage. "Excuse me? You're the one who lied. You made horrible assumptions about me and you lied about who you were and what you wanted and you're trying to take me to task because I didn't send a thank-you note?"

"I…"

She stood, which forced him to his feet.

"You lied," she repeated. "I don't do liars. I could have handled pretty much anything else, but no. That would have been too easy."

"You were there because of the money," he said, in a feeble attempt to defend himself. Apologizing hadn't worked—maybe she would respond to an offense better than defense.

"Oh, please. I was there because I recently discovered I had a grandmother and I'm still thinking I want to have a relationship with her. It was never about the money and you know it." She folded her arms over her chest. "That's what gets me the most, Ryan. You know all of that. We had a great connection. That night was…" She paused and swallowed. "Forget it."

"Julie, don't do this. Don't shut me out. You're right. It *was* a great night. Magic. That doesn't happen very often in my life. What about yours? Are you really going to walk away from that because of a mistake?"

She glared at him. "A mistake is losing your keys. You lied about who you were with the express purpose of hurting me. Magic or not, those aren't qualities I look for in a man."

Right. "So why are you here?"

She sucked in a breath, then stared him in the eye. "I'm pregnant. We had sex and we didn't use anything. Didn't even discuss it, which is pretty dumb, but there we are. My excuse is I haven't been in a relationship for over a year and wasn't on anything. I won't presume to know what your excuse is."

He heard the words, but they didn't mean anything. His body froze and his brain stopped working.

Pregnant…as in *pregnant*?

"How?" he asked before he could stop himself. He shook his head. "Never mind. I know the answer to that."

"How comforting."

Pregnant. He couldn't comprehend what that meant. Sure, having kids had always been something he'd known would happen eventually, but now? Like this? With a woman who hated him?

The timing sucked the big one, but a baby? He found himself kind of liking the idea.

Julie sat down. She would have preferred to stay standing, but these days she was always at risk of being a little woozy. Some women could go their entire pregnancy without feeling symptoms. She'd managed to get her first one less than a month after conception. Was that just her luck?

Only she couldn't be upset. Even as Ryan stood there looking shocked and ready to bolt, she couldn't be unhappy. Not about having a child.

"I wasn't sure if I should even tell you," she said, probably shocking him with her honesty, but she had no choice. She was a big fan of the truth. "I've debated for the past two days. But you are the father and you have the right to know." She drew in a breath. "Just so we're all clear, I'm keeping the baby."

"I'm glad."

Really? Color her surprised. But then what did she really know about Ryan?

Except that he was a liar, of course.

"You can sign away your rights and I'll take full responsibility," she said, wondering if he would. It was the easy out, the most practical. Most men would jump at the chance. A week ago, she would have assumed *she* would have jumped at the chance.

But something had happened. The second Dr. Greenberg had said she was pregnant, Julie's heart had nearly burst with joy. She'd never much thought about having children. They had been far in her future. Yet knowing there was a life growing inside of her had changed everything. In that moment, she'd suddenly felt her life had meaning and purpose, which theoretically it had had before, but not in such a big way.

A baby. No, a miracle.

He braced his arms on the table and leaned toward her. "No," he said clearly. "I *will* be a father to my child."

Great. Because morning sickness wasn't enough of a hassle. "You don't have to do this to look good. No one needs to know."

His dark gaze locked with hers. "I will be a father to my child," he said again, his voice low and forceful. "I *want* to."

He looked good. Too good. She hated that she still found him tempting. She wanted to lean toward him as well, so their mouths were close. She wanted to breathe in the scent of him and touch him and be touched. She wanted him to make the bad parts of their last time together go away so they could have the good parts again and again.

"Obviously we'll have to work something out," she said calmly so he wouldn't guess what she'd been thinking. "As I'm less than a month along, we have time to deal with all this."

She rose and pulled a business card out of her jacket pocket. She'd put it there earlier and had written her home number on the back. Of course she'd hoped he would agree to walk away from the child, but based on how her luck was going lately, it hadn't seemed likely.

She held out the card.

"That's it?" he asked.

"What do you mean?"

"You have nothing else to say? Nothing else you want to talk about?"

She set her card on the table and shrugged. "There isn't anything else. I'm pregnant. That's for me to deal with. When there's a child, you can get involved. Between now and then, I suppose we'll talk."

"You mean I'll call and you'll ignore my messages."

She thought about the times he'd phoned her office. "I won't ignore them this time."

"I'm not sure I believe that."

She picked up her purse. "I'm not the one who lies."

"Are you ever going to let that go?"

"No."

He took a step toward her. "Julie, we're having a baby together. You have to forgive me sometime."

"Actually, I don't," she said, then turned on her heel and left.

Six

Ryan spent the afternoon in his office, not working.

Pregnant. He knew he'd been there and he knew what had happened, but it still seemed impossible that a single night could produce a baby.

Todd walked in and slumped on the leather sofa by the window.

"So what did she want?" he asked, then shook his head. "No, wait. I want to guess. She's forgiven all and desperately wants to be with you."

"Did she act like either of those was true?"

Todd shrugged. "She was mad, sure, but was it real or an act? Come on. We've seen it all. Some of them are better than others."

At one time Ryan would have agreed with his cousin.

Recently he'd become convinced there weren't any honest women left. But he'd been wrong.

"She's pregnant."

Todd straightened and stared at him. Then he swore and flopped back on the sofa. "You're totally screwed," he said glumly. "Doesn't it just figure. She wins in the end."

"No one's winning," Ryan said. "We're dealing. She asked me if I wanted to sign away rights."

"And in return she'd ask you for nothing?" Todd shook his head. "I won't believe it until I see the paperwork myself."

"I told her no."

"Of course you did."

"This isn't what I would have planned, but now that it's happened…" He didn't know what to say. In truth, the thought of a kid of his own was appealing.

Todd frowned. "Don't go all father and son on me."

"I wouldn't mind a daughter."

Todd groaned.

Ryan grinned. "Look at the bright side. I read somewhere that a child gets most of its intelligence from the mother. Julie's bright enough that her kid could grow up to save the world."

"*You* need saving right now. You barely know this woman and now you're having a baby with her? If she offered you an out, you need to think about taking it."

"No."

"Look what happened last time."

"This is different. I won't be a stepfather. I'll be involved from the beginning. We'll make decisions together."

"You sure about that?"

"Julie has every right to be pissed at me."

"I don't agree but we'll go with it," Todd said. "Fine. She's pissed and are you so sure she'll get over it? Or play straight with you? Are you even sure the kid is yours?"

Ryan stared at his cousin. "Have you always been such a cynical bastard?"

"We both are."

"Not anymore."

"No way." Todd rested one ankle on the opposite knee. "You can't tell me this changes anything. You met her, you liked her, you obviously slept with her, which I'll now point out you didn't tell me."

"It didn't seem relevant."

"All evidence to the contrary. You have no way of knowing who she was with the night or week before she met you. Okay, sure, assume it's yours, but protect yourself, Ryan. It makes sense."

It did make sense, he thought. The thing was, he knew it wasn't necessary. Something in his gut told him that Julie was telling the truth.

"Maybe she planned this," Todd said. "Maybe she set the whole thing up."

"Right. She arranged to reconcile with a grandmother she didn't know she had, confident Ruth would insist one of the sisters go out on a date with you. Then she waited until the perfect night of her cycle, arranged the date, seduced me, dragged me home and slept with me without knowing if I would use a condom, all the while hoping she would get knocked up."

"It could happen," Todd muttered.

"You're making me rethink our partnership."

"I'm looking out for you. I know you, Ryan. You have that damned honorable streak. You keep it hidden, but I know it's there. You lied to her and even though you were justified and angry at the time, you hate that you did it. Now the woman is pregnant and you're feeling responsible. Don't be stupid."

"I won't be."

"Like I believe that. At least don't do anything until after the kid is born and you get a DNA test, okay? I can get you the name of a good lawyer."

Ryan appreciated Todd's intentions, but they weren't necessary. "Julie *is* a good lawyer."

"I meant the name of one who isn't out to screw you."

Unfortunately Ryan doubted Julie would ever want that again. He'd spent their brief meeting thinking about getting her naked again and he would bet money that she'd been planning fifty ways to skin him alive.

"Are you sure she isn't in it for the money?" Todd asked.

"Yes."

"I'm not. Ryan you're the closest thing I'll ever have to a brother. Remember what happened last time. I don't want you worked over again."

"Julie wouldn't do that."

"How do you know?"

Ryan didn't have an answer. It was something he felt, not something he could prove or explain.

In truth, Todd had a point. Ryan knew very little about Julie. It was possible she was just in it for the money. Maybe this was a game to her. But honest to God, he couldn't begin to care if she was.

Which said what about him?

"She's not like that," he said at last.

Todd shook his head. "They're all like that."

"Why am I meeting you here?" Willow asked as she climbed out of her car and glanced around at the shopping center. As Julie had requested, she'd parked in front of the office-supply store. "Is there a sale on paper clips or colored pens?"

Julie waited until her sister had joined her on the sidewalk. "I have something to tell you."

"You don't want to be a lawyer anymore? You're going into retail?"

"Almost."

"Don't make any big decisions now, while you're still in recovery from jerk-man. He's not worth it."

"I appreciate the support."

Delicate little Willow was also so passionate about everything. Unfortunately, when guys looked at her, they tended to see a best friend or a buddy. But one day the right man would open his eyes and be swept away. Julie hoped he was up for the ride.

"So I have something to tell you," Julie said as she led her sister past the office-supply center and toward the baby store next door. "I left out a small detail of my night with Ryan."

"He's a hermaphrodite?" Willow asked with a grin. "Because that would have made things really weird."

"More weird than you know." Julie faced her and

stared into blue eyes that were so much like her own. "I slept with him."

Willow surprised her by nodding slowly. "I kind of figured that."

"What? How? I didn't say anything." Julie had always thought she was *good* at keeping secrets. "I didn't even hint."

"You didn't have to. You were more upset than you needed to be and that's more my flaw or even Marina's. Not yours. So I figured there had to be a reason. Sleeping with Ryan was the most logical."

Julie sighed. Her sisters knew her and she knew them. That was at the core of their closeness. "I'd been looking forward to your shock and outrage."

"I could get huffy now, if that would help."

"I appreciate that, but I'm okay. Still, there's one more thing." She motioned to the baby store.

This time she got the reaction she'd been expecting before. Willow turned slowly, then froze in place. Her eyes widened, her mouth dropped open and she gave a strangled sound.

"You're pregnant," she breathed. "Oh no. Pregnant? Really? By Ryan?"

"Uh-huh. It was a busy night." Julie went for humor because if she actually sat down and thought about the mess she was in, she got overwhelmed.

"Pregnant." Willow reached for her hand. "What do you think? Are you happy?"

Julie smiled. "Yeah, I really am. I never thought much about kids except as something to get to later, but the second I found out, I knew I wanted this baby."

"Have you told Ryan?"

"Yesterday."

"What did he say?"

"Not much of anything. He looked a little shell-shocked, then said we needed to talk. We exchanged business cards."

Willow frowned. "That's it? Shouldn't there have been more?"

"I don't know." Julie felt unsettled about her conversation with him, but she couldn't figure out why. "He wasn't expecting to see me again, so under the circumstances he did okay. The baby threw him, but then it threw me, too. We'll deal with things when we have to. I offered to let him sign away his responsibilities, but he refused."

She hadn't really expected him to accept, which was strange. Wouldn't a man who felt comfortable lying to a woman he'd never met about whom he was and then sleeping with her seem the perfect candidate for baby abandonment?

"So you're in this together," Willow said.

"Sort of. Until there's an actual baby, I don't plan to hang out with him much."

Willow squeezed her arm. "A baby. Are you excited?"

"Yes. I am. Scared, too, but mostly excited."

"I get to be an aunt and buy presents and babysit." Willow's hold on her arm tightened. "Maybe it was supposed to happen this way. Maybe he's your—"

Julie groaned. "Don't say it, I beg you. Ryan is not my destiny."

"But you never know."

"I know. Now, come on. Let's go look at baby furniture. We have a nursery to plan."

"Your eleven o'clock is here," Leah said as she poked her head into Julie's office. "Cute guy."

Julie smiled at her assistant—the one she shared with two other second-year associates. "Do you tell that sort of thing to Mark and James?"

"Mark, no," Leah said cheerfully. "But there are rumors about James, so he might be interested if you're not."

"You're bad."

"Yes, I am. In every way possible."

Leah was a fifty-something grandmother who was also a brilliant assistant. She'd been with the firm longer than most senior partners and refused to work for any of them, contending that the associates needed her more. She'd been invaluable to Julie on more than one occasion.

Julie glanced at her calendar and saw the next hour blocked simply by a "potential client" notation. No name, no stated reason for the appointment. Interesting. Leah usually filled in the details.

Julie picked up a legal pad, her pen and BlackBerry, then walked down the long corridor to the main foyer.

As she stepped onto the polished marble floor by the round reception desk, she came to a stop so quickly, her feet nearly slid out from under her.

Ryan Bennett stood talking to Ethan Jackson, a senior partner in the firm.

Her psyche neatly split in two with her body and her emotions sighing at the sight of Ryan and her brain wanting to spit fire.

He could *not* be her potential new client, she thought frantically. How on earth could she do business with the man who had lied about who he was, slept with her and was now the father of her unborn child? That wasn't anyone's life—that was a movie-of-the-week plot.

It wasn't fair. It wasn't right. If he thought he could weasel his way into her world with a big check to her law firm then he… Damn, then he was right.

His venture-capital company was big business and it was her job to help the firm's bottom line. Second-year associates who wanted to make it to partner didn't turn down millions of dollars in billing for personal reasons. Assuming that's what he was here for.

She sucked in a deep breath, vowed she would ignore how good he looked in his suit and how much she remembered about his mouth on her body, stepped forward and smiled.

"Good morning, Ethan."

Both men turned to her.

"Julie," Ethan said as he nodded. "Good. You have a new client here. Ryan Bennett, meet Julie Nelson."

"We've met," Julie said, wanting to get everything out in the open. Well, everything except the fact that she'd slept with Ryan on their first and only date and was now pregnant. Talk about tacky.

"That's right," Ryan said easily. "We're almost related. My great-aunt by marriage is Julie's grandmother. Due to some family estrangements, we only met a few weeks ago."

Ethan gave her an approving glance. She was sure her

relationship with Ryan would be discussed at the next partner meeting and a little star would go next to her name.

"I'm here to talk about our business in China," Ryan continued. "We have several companies looking to get 'the China price' on various items, along with some companies wanting to do manufacturing there. I'm hoping your expertise can make a difference."

Ethan looked happier than Julie had ever seen him. "Then I'll leave you two to get this going. Let me know how you progress, Julie."

"Of course," she said, holding in a sigh. If Ryan was serious about bringing that much business to the firm, they would be working very closely together. The thought of that closeness made her uncomfortable and far too aware of him.

"Let's step into a conference room," she said and led the way.

When the glass paneled door was carefully shut and she'd offered both coffee and bottled water, which he refused, she took a seat across from his.

"What's this all about?" she asked, keeping her voice low, her expression controlled. This particular room had mostly glass walls. She'd chosen it deliberately, so that they would both be forced to keep things polite.

"I told you. When we had dinner, you mentioned you dealt with international concerns and that you speak Mandarin. It seemed like a good fit."

"Are you setting me up?" she asked bluntly. "Do you plan to dangle all these billable hours in front of me and one of the partners, only to pull them back later? Whatever you may think, I didn't get pregnant on purpose. If your plan is to get me fired, thinking then you'll have an easier time manipulating me, you can forget it. I'm one of the best lawyers you'll ever come up against and I won't let you mess things up for me."

He swore under his breath. "Is that what you think? That I'm doing this to set you up? That it's a joke?"

"I don't know. You're the one who decided I deserved to be taught a lesson. Why shouldn't I think the worst?"

"Did it ever occur to you I might be here to do business? That I'm accepting what I did was wrong and even though I've apologized that doesn't begin to make it right. Did it occur to you that I'm doing my best to make a difficult situation easier for both of us, but mostly you. We need a good international lawyer. Todd and I were discussing that and I thought of you. That's it. No hidden agenda."

It was a good speech, but was he telling the truth? "I want to believe you," she said.

"So give it a try." He leaned forward. "Julie, why would I want to set you up? Why would I want to hurt you any more than I have? I know this is going to be difficult for you to believe, but I'm actually a pretty decent guy."

She raised her eyebrows. "You lied."

"Yes, I did. It was a moment of bad judgment. Ever have one of those?"

She touched her stomach. "Maybe."

"You can't keep running from me."

"As you're sitting across from me," she said, "I'm not running."

"You know what I mean. Look, I'm here to talk to you about helping us out. Strictly business. I've checked around and you're good at what you do. I need someone good. If, in the process, we have a chance to get to know each other in a less charged situation, isn't that for the best?"

"I guess." He was being so logical and rational. Normally she appreciated that. But along with the wooziness, she seemed to be fighting some pretty impressive mood swings. "If you're sincere about the business—"

"I am."

"Then let's talk."

"Good. Okay."

He smiled. It shouldn't have meant anything. Men smiled all the time. But there was something about Ryan's smile, about the way he stared into her eyes, as if she had his full attention. He made her knees go weak and she wasn't even standing.

"Is that offer for coffee still open?" he asked.

"Sure. How do you take it?"

"Black."

She stood and shook her head. "Such a typical guy."

"Of course. Come on. Admit it—you'd have no respect for me if I asked for three sugars and hazelnut flavored cream."

That made her laugh. "You're right. I'll be back."

"I'll come with you."

"You don't have to." Her plan had been to escape for a minute and get herself together. Having him tag along would make the whole "get together" bit complicated.

But there was no polite way to say no, so she led him

into the break room and grabbed a clean mug from the tray by the full coffeepot.

"You don't have staff?" he asked.

"I do, but I prefer not to waste her time on errands. The other two associates I share her with don't agree with my position." She glanced at him over her shoulder. "Leah likes me much better."

"I'm sure she does."

He smiled again and Julie found herself caught up in the moment. Unfortunately, she was pouring coffee at the time and when the mug was full, the hot liquid poured over the sides and onto her hand.

"Ouch!"

She set the mug on the counter and shook off her hand, her skin burning. Suddenly Ryan was at her side. He took the pot from her, then nudged her over to the sink. While standing behind her, he took her injured hand in his and held it under the cold water.

"I didn't know you were a klutz," he said conversationally.

"I'm not usually."

She wasn't. She'd been distracted. She still was.

He stood right behind her—his front pressing against her back. She could feel the strength and power of his body, along with the heat.

Warmth seeped into her, making her want to sigh and rub and stroke. She could feel his fingers on her hand, his arm pressing against her. He was leaning forward, his face right next to hers.

If she turned just a little bit to the right, their mouths would be inches apart.

She wanted to kiss him. It didn't matter that she practically hated him, she still felt longing building up inside of her.

Just one kiss. It didn't have to last very long. Just mouths pressing, tongues stroking, bodies—

She jerked her hand free and stepped to the side. "I'm good. Thanks."

She pulled a paper towel from the holder and dried her hand, then mopped up the spill on the counter. After collecting a bottle of water for herself, she led the way back to the conference room.

Her insides felt soft and mushy. Her panties were damp and that place between her thighs was swollen and achy.

Pathetic, she thought grimly as she sat down and tried to gather her thoughts together. She was deeply pathetic. How could he have reduced her to a puddle after just one night? Sure, it had been a great night, but she'd had great nights before.

Well, not that great. But still.

She reached for her pen. "Why don't you outline what you have in mind," she said.

Ryan began to talk about the business. Julie took notes, but she wasn't really listening. How could he be so unaffected by what had just happened? Wouldn't that be horrible—if the attraction was all one-sided? Life couldn't possibly be that unfair.

"We provide venture capital and retain a major interest in each of our companies. The goal is to take them all public, but when that doesn't happen, we sometimes sell them. Right now there are three specific firms I need help with. Two are looking to do business with

China, while the third is perfect for overseas manufacturing. I assume you have contacts in China."

She looked at him. Now it was her turn to smile. "Of course. Personal as well as professional."

"Want to explain that?"

"We had a neighbor when I was growing up. Mrs. Wu had been a teacher. She retired only to discover she was bored with too much time on her hands. She taught my sisters and I Mandarin. I'm the only one who was really interested. When I was in high school, she took me to China with her to visit her family. I went back the following two summers and did a semester in China during college."

"Impressive."

"Thank you."

"What happens now?" he asked. "You'll want specific information on the companies."

"Absolutely. Also what, if anything, you've already done to establish relationships in China. We'll work on a retainer agreement, with my time billed in quarter-hour segments."

"Seems reasonable."

"I'll want a substantial sum up front."

She would ask for more than the firm usually suggested, mostly to cover her butt.

He sipped his coffee. "You still don't trust me."

"I'm willing to give you the benefit of the doubt, but I'm not willing to be stupid." No matter how her body reacted to him.

"Fair enough." His dark gaze settled on her face. "Todd and I are both only children. We grew up spending a lot of time together. We became as close as brothers."

"A bit of a non sequitur, but okay. And I already know this part. It's why you agreed to do his dirty work."

He ignored her. "We grew up rich. From the time we were teenagers there were girls, then later women, willing to do anything to get close. They weren't interested in us—they wanted the money."

"I refuse to believe every female you've ever met has ignored who you are in favor of your bank account."

"Not everyone, but enough. Under the circumstances, knowing what our aunt had promised you and your sisters, it wasn't unreasonable I think that about you."

Julie opened her mouth, then closed it. Okay, maybe she could see his point. "I know what it looks like, but that isn't the way it is."

"I believe you. Can you do the same? Can you possibly understand why Todd and I might suspect you weren't any different?"

"I don't know. Maybe. So don't go on the date. Refuse. Setting up a stranger to teach her a lesson to punish her for every other bitchy female you've met isn't right."

"Agreed. So you *can* see my side?"

He was starting to get on her nerves. What did he want? "Yes, your childhood was very tragic. Poor rich boys liked by millions for all the wrong reasons."

"You're not easy."

"I don't try to be. I've said I'll try to understand why you thought the worst of me and I'll accept your apology for what you did, but that doesn't mean I approve of it or even understand your actions. I still don't trust you."

"You're going to have to try. We'll be a family."

On what planet? "Not under any definition I can think of. We'll be co-parenting a child. That doesn't make us a family."

"You can call it what you want," he told her, "but having a baby together makes us a family. Everything has changed, Julie. There's more here than what each of us feels. There's a third life. Our child deserves the best from us. That's why I think we should get married."

Seven

"Married?" Julie sprang to her feet and stared down at Ryan. "Are you insane? *Married?* What the hell is wrong with you?"

She suddenly remembered the glass walls and sat down again. She lowered her voice, but she wasn't any less pissed off.

"If this is your idea of a joke, it's not funny. It's horrible." Married? What was he thinking? And just when she'd decided he might not be so awful after all.

"Horrible?" he asked, sounding disgustingly calm. "How so?"

"We don't even *like* each other," she muttered. "What about being married would be pleasant?"

"I do like you," he said. "Aside from a single act you

can't forgive, I think you like me. Getting married for the sake of a baby is a time-honored tradition."

"In what century?"

Had he really said he liked her? She shook her head. She had to get a grip. Who cared if he liked her? She would never marry Ryan—not in her lifetime.

"We're rational, intelligent adults," Ryan said. "We're having a baby together. We'll both want our child to have the best of everything and that means having both parents around. Do you really want to be a single mother?"

"Yes. I'm fine with it. I was raised by a single mother." Sort of. Technically there was a father, but it wasn't as if he'd ever bothered to stay more than fifteen minutes at a time.

"I think it's important to have both parents around if at all possible," he told her.

"Great, but it's not possible."

"Why?"

Why? She hated that he was sitting there, discussing this, all cool and composed while she was wishing they were in the law library so she could throw some really heavy books at his head.

"I don't want to marry you," she said, making her words as clear as possible.

"Why not?"

She was going to kill him and it wasn't going to be her fault. "I don't know you. Despite what your ego-inflated brain tells you, I don't particularly like you. I'm not interested in getting married for some arcane sociological reason and I think a single parent can do a perfectly excellent job."

"We could try."

What was with him? Why did he keep pushing? And why was she both furious and incredibly sad?

"I don't want to try. Not with you."

"Okay. So it's not me," he said. "You object to marriage in general."

"I do not. I want to get married. Someday." When men stopped lying to her. "Just not now and not to you. You're a man who assumes all women are after his money. I couldn't stand that."

"You're saying you'd object to a prenuptial agreement? Protecting my assets is only reasonable."

Right now he should be a whole lot more worried about his ass than his assets, she thought grimly as she briefly glanced around, looking for something sharp so she could stab him.

"You need to go," she said between gritted teeth. "Seriously, I have work to do. I know you don't understand how I could possibly turn down your incredibly flattering offer. Based on your view of women, there must be thousands who would take the plunge, especially after such a romantic proposal. Be still my heart. Wait. It is."

One corner of his mouth twitched, as if he found this funny. That made her want to grind him into dust.

"So much energy," he said in an infuriatingly soothing tone. "Makes me wonder what you're hiding. Getting married isn't all that unexpected a concept, Julie. So what are you really upset about?"

She stood. "This has been fabulous. We should do it again. Maybe have a party, exchange gift bags."

He stood and walked around to her side of the table, took her hand and pushed her back into a corner of the room. One where they were out of sight of anyone walking by.

"I'm not going to leave this alone," he said, staring into her eyes and making her thighs whimper. "Whatever you say, whatever you do, I'm sticking around. This is my child and my life, too. Don't think you can hide from me forever."

Then he kissed her. Right there in the office, in front of an empty conference table and a display cabinet holding some very expensive crystal pieces.

He pressed his lips to hers in a move that was both erotic and possessive. The heat was as instantaneous as it was intense. Her fingers itched to grab hold of him and never let go. The rest of her body just wanted to be naked and plastered against his.

She fought against her desire to deepen the kiss, but before she could either win or lose the battle, he stepped back.

"Have the paperwork drawn up for the retainer agreement and sent over to my office," he said. "I'll messenger it back with a check."

What? Oh, yeah. Work. "I'm not interested in working with you."

"Maybe not, but you want the account, so you'll suffer. And Julie?"

She carefully wiped her mouth with her fingers before answering. "Yes?"

"How ever much you try to deny it—I know the truth. You *do* like me."

* * *

"I love bagels," Marina said as she emptied the bag. "I love the smell of them toasting, slathering them with cream cheese, taking them out onto the patio and eating one while sipping coffee and reading the Sunday paper."

Julie glanced at Willow. "Okay, I'm suddenly hungry. How about you?"

"Starved. Mom won't be back for another half hour or so. We could snack."

"There's plenty to choose from."

In one of those unexpected quirks of fate, Julie had finished up all her work on Friday and hadn't had to go into the office on Saturday morning. With nothing to fill her time except brooding, she decided to go to the farmer's market and wander around. She'd indulged herself with tons of fresh fruits and vegetables, a sinfully gooey Danish and a baker's dozen of fresh bagels that she'd shared with her sisters.

Marina pulled out the three bagels she would take home with her and put them in a separate bag. "So how are you feeling?"

"Good."

"Not that I need to know," Marina continued as if her sister hadn't spoken. "I'm used to you keeping things from me."

Julie groaned. "I invited you to join Willow and me last week, but you had that microbiology class."

"Inorganic chemistry, but thanks for being interested."

"Marina, come on. I told you as soon as you got home."

"Yes, you did." Her sister smiled at her. "So I still love you."

"Great. Another conditional relationship. What happened to unconditional love forever?"

"We put it in the recycling bin," Willow said helpfully. "It's too late to get it back. They've already picked up." She dumped the container of blueberries that had cost a fortune from the colander into a bowl. "Berry?"

"Thanks." Julie grabbed a handful as she sank onto a stool by the center island.

"What's wrong?" Marina asked. "You seem, I don't know, not yourself."

"I'm fine. Sort of."

Willow wrinkled her nose. "That doesn't sound good. Are you sick? Too much queasiness?"

"No. I can handle that. It's just…" Julie hadn't decided if she was going to mention Ryan's stupid proposal, but suddenly she couldn't keep it to herself.

"He came to see me yesterday," she began.

"Ryan?" Marina asked helpfully.

Julie nodded. "He made an appointment. He's dangling his company's China business in front of me and I don't like it. One of the partners met him and now sees flashing dollar signs. It would be a lot in billable hours."

"Which sounds good," Willow said cautiously. "So what's the problem?"

"I don't trust him. What if he's just playing another sick, twisted game? What if he sets this all up and then disappears, taking his billable hours with him? I would look stupid in front of the partners. It wouldn't be good for my career."

Marina and Willow glanced at each other and then at her.

"Um, don't take this wrong," Willow said quietly, "but why would he do that? What does he have to gain?"

"I don't know. Just to screw with me. Don't forget this was a guy intent on teaching me a lesson, even though he'd never met me and knew nothing about me."

"That was wrong," Marina said. "But this is totally different. Julie, I can't believe he wants to hurt your career. You're having a baby together—why would he want to hurt the mother of his child?"

"To get control. That's all he cares about."

Julie knew she didn't sound exactly rational, but she couldn't seem to keep a grip on her emotions. "I just…" She swallowed and found herself fighting tears. "Okay, I'm weak. That's it, the truth in all its ickiness. I know better than to expect a guy to be decent. I know better than to dream about someone who's honest and caring. I know I should let the romantic dreams go and I try. I really try. But then when I least expect it, they pop back up and I'm hopeful and then the hopes get crushed and I want to slap myself for being so stupid in the first place."

"I love you like a sister," Willow said, which made Julie almost smile. "But what on earth are you talking about?"

"He asked me to marry him."

"Okay, then," Marina said, sliding on to the stool next to Julie's. "Start at the beginning and talk slowly."

Willow pushed aside the berries and leaned against the counter. "You have our full attention. I promise."

"There's not much to tell," Julie said with a sigh. "He came to the office yesterday."

She explained how Ryan had spoken about his three companies and how they needed help. "Then somehow we were talking about personal stuff, how he and Todd were close when they grew up and how women only wanted them for their money."

"It could happen," Marina said.

"Poor little rich boys," Willow muttered sarcastically.

"That's what I told him. Anyway, we were talking about that and then he said we should get married. That it was the best thing for the baby." She paused, then shrugged. "I didn't take it well."

"Why?" Willow asked.

"Because… He really ticked me off. You don't propose just like that. It's wrong. We barely know each other. I don't trust him and, based on how he treated me, he doesn't trust me. It's not exactly a basis for a successful marriage. I got angry."

"I get it," Willow told her. "He violated those secret dreams you're not supposed to have. It wasn't romantic and perfect and he doesn't love you."

"I refuse to have a weak side," Julie said. "I'm tough."

"You're human," Willow said.

"But it *was* romantic," Marina said.

Julie rolled her eyes. "Here we go."

"It's true," her baby sister insisted. "You get married because you have to, then you fall madly in love. It's fabulous."

"She's insane," Julie muttered.

"At least he was willing to do the right thing," Willow said. "I know he was totally in the wrong on your date. Lying like that. But you know, I kind of don't totally blame him. It's really that Todd Aston's fault. He's the one who was too big a jerk to show up and talk to you himself."

Julie thought they were both rats. "Ryan had his own agenda. Don't make him into the hero of the night."

"I won't, but maybe there's a chance he's not all bad."

"A tiny one."

"So you won't consider his proposal?" Marina asked.

"Not even on a bet. It would be dumb to marry a man I barely know just because I'm pregnant."

There was a sound from the doorway. Julie looked up to find her mother standing there.

This was *so* not how she wanted to tell the news.

Willow and Marina disappeared into the back of the house. Julie stayed on her stool and watched her mother make coffee.

"It's decaf," Naomi Nelson said as she flipped on the switch.

"Thanks."

Her mother turned to face her.

Naomi had run away with her one true love when she'd been just eighteen. She'd been pregnant and Julie's birth had been followed by two more babies in the next two years. Naomi had been all of twenty-five the first time her husband had left.

Julie remembered very little of that day, except her mother's crying. She'd been six and had just started the first grade. She'd brought home a picture she'd done in class, but her mother had been too sad to look at it. From that day on, she'd never been able to work on a school art project without remembering her mother's tears.

"So," her mother said calmly. "What's new?"

"Oh, Mom. I'm sorry. I didn't mean for you to find out that way."

"Did you mean for me to find out at all? You're pregnant, Julie, and you didn't tell me."

Naomi was slim, pretty and not yet fifty. Yet suddenly, she looked older than Julie had ever seen her. Her blue eyes were dark with emotion, but hurt rather than anger.

"I'm sorry," Julie repeated. "I was going to, I just didn't know how to say the words. I didn't plan this. In fact I messed up big time."

"Did you think I'd judge you?" her mother asked. "When have I ever done that?"

Julie shifted uncomfortably on the chair. "I don't usually screw up like this."

"Then you'll need some help getting through it. What happened?"

"I went on the date with Todd."

Her mother shook her head. "I thought you girls had decided not to do that."

"We had, but it seemed so important to Ruth and it was only one date." Julie stopped. "Mom, no one blames you for what happened with your mother."

Ruth had not approved of Naomi's relationship with Jack Nelson. When Naomi had run off with him, Ruth had cut her daughter out of her life.

"I appreciate that. I don't blame myself either. So the baby is Todd's?"

"Not exactly." Julie explained how Ryan had taken Todd's place and how she'd been swept away. "He wanted to teach me a lesson. He was playing me for a fool. Now he says he's sorry and he thinks we should try to have a relationship. Honestly, how can I ever trust the guy?"

Her mother was quiet for a few seconds. "I don't know if you can. Do you want to?"

Did she? "Maybe. Sometimes. I don't know. We're having a baby together—there's a complication." Julie stopped and smiled. "Mom, I'm having a baby."

Her mother moved close and hugged her. "I know. How do you feel? Are you happy?"

Julie leaned back and touched her arm. "I am thrilled beyond words. I never thought about having kids except in the abstract, but now that I'm pregnant, I'm really excited. I want this child. I can't believe how much."

"You were never one to explore your softer side," her mother said. "You always felt you had to be in charge and take care of everyone else. There wasn't a whole lot of energy left over for you to think about yourself. I'm glad you want the baby. You're going to be a wonderful mother."

The unexpected praise made her eyes fill with tears.

"Thanks," she murmured, feeling awkward and grateful at the same time. "You're my role model. You did great with us. We can't have been easy, what with you on your own."

As soon as she said the words, she wanted to call them back.

"I wasn't on my own," her mother said. "Your father was here."

"A few weeks a year," Julie said before she could stop herself. "Mom, come on. I know you love him, but he wasn't a good husband or a good father."

Her mother bristled. "He's still your father. You will talk about him with respect."

"Why? I don't get it. I've never understood why you let him come and go as he pleases."

"It's your father's nature. He's restless. But that doesn't make him a bad man."

"It doesn't make him a good one either."

Julie wondered why she bothered. They'd had this same discussion a hundred times before. She would never understand how her mother could give her heart to a man who thought so little of her that he would disappear for months at a time. Then he'd return with gifts and wild stories, staying just long enough to convince everyone that this time was different, that this time he would stay. Only he never did.

Julie had stopped believing in him a long time ago but her mother led with her heart.

"He's not a man to be tied down," her mother said quietly. "I've accepted that. I wish you could. This will always be his home and I will always be his wife."

"I can't do that. I can't understand him and I won't forgive him."

"Having a child changes you," her mother told her. "It changes everything."

Julie knew it wouldn't change her enough to see her father's view of the world, but that didn't matter. She shifted the subject to something less divisive.

"Ryan thinks we should get married," she said.

"What do you think?"

"That he's crazy. We've had one date. Okay, it went really well until he admitted he was a lying rat, but that's not enough to build a life on." She looked at her mother. "You're going to tell me I should marry him, aren't you?"

"I'm going to say that he's your baby's father and that you need to meet him at least halfway."

"What if I don't want to?"

Her mother smiled. "That's mature. I'm so proud."

"Mo-om."

"Julie, life is about compromise. What Ryan did was wrong. If he's really the jerk you say, then why is he going to all this trouble to convince you he's sorry? Jerks don't bother with things like that. And how is marrying you a win for him? If he was only interested in the victory, he's already slept with you."

"Ouch."

"I'm just saying that men who are into the conquest for the sake of numbers don't hang around. He's hung around. He says he wants to be a father to his child. That's not a bad thing. You don't have to marry him. You don't have to do anything. But you might want to think about getting to know him. Start there and see where it goes. Maybe he's secretly a good man."

"You think?" Julie asked. "With my luck?"

Her mother's words made sense, but Julie so didn't want to go there. She wanted to stay mad. It was safer. Getting to know Ryan meant putting herself at risk. What if she started to believe in him? He would only hurt her.

"Not every man is Garrett," her mother said.

"You want to bet?"

Eight

Ryan lived in a high rise condo that was all glass and steel. Julie was sure there had to be more to the construction because this was L.A. and earthquakes were a certainty. Regardless of what high-tech innovation kept the building standing, she was unimpressed by the modern coldness of it all. Sure, the location was great and the concierge service would take care of all the details of life, but she preferred her slightly scruffy neighborhood where lawns were normal and kids played on the sidewalk.

Of course being critical of Ryan's building was a fabulous distraction, she admitted as she stepped off the elevator and walked down the hall to his condo. She'd decided to take her mother's advice from the previous weekend and get to know the man. She'd called him and suggested they get together, and he'd offered lunch at his place.

She rang the bell. He answered right away.

He seemed taller than she remembered, but maybe her brain was fuzzy from the shock of seeing him in casual clothes. The designer suit was gone. In its place were worn and faded jeans and a long-sleeved white shirt. Both emphasized his lean strength.

His shirt was open at the collar, exposing a tanned chest and a light dusting of hair. She remembered touching him there, running her hands across his warm skin and feeling him react to her caress. Of course she'd pretty much touched him everywhere, and that memory playground was a place she wanted to avoid.

"You made it," he said. "Come on in."

"It wasn't that hard to find."

"I thought you might change your mind," he admitted. "After last time."

Right. Last time. Their fight in her office, because he'd proposed. Just thinking about it made her angry enough to spit, although honestly, she'd never spit in her life. But if anyone was going to make her, it was Ryan.

Still, she wasn't here to argue with him. "You said on the phone we could pretend that never happened."

He smiled. "You're right. So this is me pretending. Come on in."

He stepped back and she entered the foyer. The shock was instant. They were the only living things in a room of glass and metal.

"I think it's important we get to know each other," she told him, deciding it was polite to ignore the stark surroundings. "The baby isn't going away and neither are you. So here we are."

He smiled. "But you'd like me to go away."

"It would uncomplicate my life."

"Boring isn't better."

"I'm not talking boring," she said. "Just a few less surprises."

"I'll try to keep them at a minimum. So we're having a truce with lunch?"

"I'm willing. We'll think of it as a spicy side dish."

His dark gaze settled on her face. "Meaning I shouldn't mistake your pleasant conversation for forgiveness?"

She'd hoped they could avoid discussing what had happened, but maybe that was impossible. "I'm working on it."

"I understand. You're not easy. I respect that."

Despite her nervousness, she laughed. "Apparently I am easy. That's what got me into this position."

He took a step toward her and lowered his voice. "You're not easy—I'm irresistible."

"Why doesn't that make me feel any better?"

"I'm not sure," he said, leading the way through the foyer. "At least it feeds my ego, which I always appreciate."

"I can imagine," she murmured.

"Come on. I'll give you the tour."

She followed him out of the foyer and into an open living space. His unit was on the corner, so he had two walls of glass, giving him a perfect view of Hollywood, the Hollywood Hills and to the east, in the distance, the skyline of downtown.

Here the predominate color was gray, accented with wood tones and bright splashes of red and orange from a large canvas of very abstract art. The end tables and dining-area table were glass and steel. The sofa and chairs, a medium gray. The walls were a lighter shade of the same. The hardwood floors and leather ottoman provided the only hint of warmth.

"What do you think?" he asked.

She set her purse on an Ultrasuède-covered chair. "It's, um, very modern."

"Not your thing?"

"Not really." And based on the little she knew about Ryan, she would guess it wasn't his thing, either.

"I was dating a decorator when I moved in. She offered and I took the easy way out."

Ah, so it *wasn't* his style. Funny how that made her like him a little.

He led the way into the kitchen. It opened onto the rest of the room and was all hard surfaces done in gray. Concrete countertops, various shades of gray in the polished glass tile backsplash, stainless appliances.

"You need to get a couple of plants," Julie said as she took the bar stool he offered on the far side of the island. "Something green and bushy and alive. Aren't you afraid all this modern stuff is going to suck the life out of you?"

"It's okay," he said with a shrug. "It's easy to keep clean."

She grinned. "You would know this how?"

"The cleaning service has mentioned it a few times. That and the fact that I don't have pets."

"I'll bet you mostly eat out, you're rarely home, you

don't have big, loud parties. You're the perfect client for them."

He stood on the other side of the island and began removing things from the built-in refrigerator.

"How do you know I don't have big parties?"

"Your sofa and chairs are in perfect condition. Nothing crunchy or wet has been dropped on them. Parties are messy."

"Good point. You're right. No parties."

Just a parade of women, she would guess. Even ignoring his sob story about women coming on to him because of his money, Julie knew Ryan was impressive enough to entice the ladies all on his own.

He carried a package of raw chicken breasts, fixings for salad, basil, some jars and bottles she didn't recognize and—she blinked to make sure she wasn't seeing things—a cookie sheet with prepared bread dough on it.

Was he serious?

"You're cooking?" she asked, trying to sound less surprised than she felt.

"I said I'd make us lunch."

"I thought you meant reservations."

"Would you rather go out?"

"No. This is great. Shocking, but great."

"You don't cook?"

"I can prepare a few basics. I don't totally live on takeout and frozen dinners. But I don't make anything that requires baking or takes this many ingredients." She rested her forearms on the counter. "So what are we having?"

"A goat-cheese-and-arugula salad, followed by a

grilled-chicken sandwich with a pesto sauce on warm focaccia bread, with fresh berries and crème anglaise for dessert."

Color her hungry, she thought as her stomach gave a rumble.

"Impressive. Let me guess. You dated a chef."

"Hey, that's a little judgmental. The summer Todd and I were twenty, our parents took us on a Mediterranean cruise for a month. We would rather have hit Europe on our own, but they insisted, so we went. It was a small ship with not much to do and nearly everyone on it was retired. I think the captain was afraid Todd and I would start trouble because he arranged for daily cooking classes. I hated the first couple, but then I got into the whole thing. Now I cook."

Impressive, she thought. "And Todd?"

Ryan grinned. "He flirted with the cocktail waitress."

He turned on the oven, set a grill pan on the six-burner stove, then seasoned two chicken breasts. After collecting a small but powerful-looking food processor, he rinsed off the basil, then dried it with a towel.

"You're really cooking," she said. "I'm sorry, but this is very unusual for me."

"You should see what I can do with a potato."

It wasn't a side of him she would have expected. With his money and easy good looks, he could have spent his life ordering room service.

As he sprinkled various spices on the bread dough he'd flattened on a cookie sheet, she found herself getting caught up in the way he moved his hands—the confidence and finesse. Without wanting to, she remembered those hands on her body. For a guy who wore a suit and tie, he was very good at manual labor.

And she was an idiot. This was *not* a good time for R-rated flashbacks. She was here to get to know the father of her child. Oh, but if things were different she would be all over him like mascara on silk.

The bread went in the oven, the chicken went on the grill pan and then he walked to the refrigerator and pulled out a pitcher with a pinkish tea mixture, sliced lemons and ice cubes.

"Herbal," he said as he poured them each a glass. "No caffeine."

"Thanks." She sipped. The flavor was more citrus than tea, but it was nice. "It's good."

"I'm glad you like it."

"Okay, you win. I'm officially confused. Is this really you?" she asked.

"Want to see some ID?"

"You know what I mean. You're…"

"Normal?" he offered.

"Yes. Normal. Nothing like the high-powered entrepreneur who hates women."

He winced. "I don't hate women. I like them."

"As long as you can teach them lessons." She held up her hand. "Sorry. I'm breaking the rules. Let's just say this is an interesting side of you. And now we can move on to safer topics. Tell me about what your life was like growing up."

He eyed her as he tore up the arugula and dropped it into a bowl. "That could get me into trouble."

"How?"

"Let me count the ways. But I'll play along. Todd and I were born within a couple of months of each other so we've always been close. Our fathers are brothers, so we traveled together a lot, went to the same schools, hung out on vacations."

"Public school?" she asked sweetly, then sipped her drink. She had already guessed the answer, but she confessed she didn't mind seeing him defensive.

"Private. Prep."

"Ah."

He glared at her, then continued. "We both went to Stanford. There was some talk of Princeton or Yale, but we weren't interested. Our lives were in California. Snow was for ski vacations, not everyday life."

"Skiing in Gstaad?" she asked.

"All over. And before you start mocking me—"

"I would never do that!"

He ignored her. "I want to point out that Ruth came from money. This could have been your life, too."

"I can understand the words, but I'll admit I can't make the concept real. Mom always said her parents were dead and we believed her."

"But if things had been different…" he began.

She looked at him. "Then you and I would have grown up together. We would have been like brother and sister."

Ryan grimaced. Not exactly the direction he wanted them to go. He thought of Julie as many things, but a sister wasn't one of them.

As he worked, he kept getting distracted by her presence. She was so alive, so vibrant. It was as if she were the only color in the room.

He liked the way she challenged him, and how she tried to be fair. He also liked the way she looked in her soft pink sweater that just hinted at the curves beneath. Curves he remembered and ached to touch and taste again.

"Or maybe we would have been each other's first love," she said.

"I like that better," he told her.

"I can see it all now. The wonder and thrill of that first kiss. Going to each other's prom."

"You'd be attending a private girls school," he said with a grin. "In a uniform."

"I'm ignoring you. We would have parted tearfully before college, tried to keep in touch, but you were incapable of being faithful. I made a surprise trip to your dorm and found you with that redhead."

"Hey—why do I have to be the bad guy? I've never been unfaithful."

Her blue eyes widened slightly. "Why don't I believe that?"

"I don't know, but it's true. I have references."

She seemed to consider that for a second. "Okay, so we just drift apart. Then on our next holiday together, Todd comes on to me. You're crushed and while the two of you are fighting I run off with the brilliant computer-science major I met in the library."

"Do I live a life of bitterness and regret?"

"Maybe. But eventually you find someone. A spinster librarian who reads Emily Dickinson to you every night."

"Gee, thanks."

"Actually, you like it a lot."

"So you still hate me, huh?" he asked.

She tilted her head and her long, blond hair tumbled across her shoulder. "Not as much as I should."

He turned the chicken and shook his head. "I wish we'd met another way. I wish I'd run into you at the beach or the grocery store or at a party."

"Ryan, don't."

"Why not? We get along. We got along that first night, we're getting along now."

"I don't know how much of that first night was real and how much of it was your agenda. Who are you really?"

"I'm trying to show you." And to be patient. Her points were valid. As much as he didn't like it, he respected her right to be cautious.

"Okay, I'm good with that," she said. "I'm trying, Ryan. I'm not being difficult on purpose."

"It's just a happy by-product?"

"Kind of."

"So tell me about your life," he said. "You know all about the tragedy of my childhood."

She smiled and his gut tightened. Imagine what she could do to him if she worked at it.

"My sisters and I were pretty happy. There wasn't a lot of money and no private schools with or without uniforms, but that was fine with us."

"Your dad died?"

She paused and for the first time since arriving, looked uncomfortable.

"No, he's alive."

What was the problem? Divorce happened all the time.

"My parents are still married," she said. "They have a unique relationship. My dad is one of those guys who can't settle down. He's charming and funny and everyone wants to be around him."

Everyone but her, Ryan thought, watching the emotions play across her face. Her father had obviously hurt her.

"He disappears," she continued. "He'll show up for a few weeks, much to the delight of my mother who adores him. He'll shower us with presents and tell us stories and get involved in our lives and then he disappears. There's never any warning and more often than not, he cleans out my mom's bank account. A few months later, he sends a check for three or four times that amount. A few months after that, he shows up again and we're off."

"That had to be hard on you," Ryan said.

"It wasn't my favorite way of life. I wanted him to stay and if he couldn't stay I wanted him gone. For so long I hated how much I loved him when he was around and how awful I felt when he left. I hated seeing my sisters so sad and listening to my mother cry."

She stiffened, as if she hadn't meant to say that much. "It's better now," she said casually. "I don't get involved."

Was that true? Was Julie really able to cut herself off from her father or did she simply avoid any emotion where he was concerned?

"How does your mom handle it?" he asked.

"She loves him." Julie's expression was both indulgent and confused. "I don't get it, but she does. She's loved him from the moment she first saw him. She walked away from her family just to be with him. From that life of wealth and privilege, from her parents. Your uncle was her stepfather, but he'd been a part of her life since she'd been a baby. As far as she was concerned, he *was* her father. According to her, it was for the best. She's never looked back, never had regrets."

He checked on the bread, then removed the chicken from the grill. The salad was ready. Once the bread was done, he would make the pesto and they'd be ready to eat.

"I admire her ability to stand by her decision," he said. "That takes courage."

"I think being totally cut off from her family helped. It wasn't as if they would have welcomed her back."

"Her father wouldn't have," he told her. "But Ruth would have. She's a soft-hearted old bird. She'd bristly and tough on the outside, but inside, she's mush."

"I haven't seen that side of her. She was pretty intimidating when she came to visit."

He smiled. "You? Intimidated? I don't believe it."

She laughed. "Okay, I was nervous. You obviously care about her. I can hear it in your voice. I mean this in the nicest possible way—why? She tried to get one of us to marry your cousin by bribing us. That's not exactly sweet."

"But it's vintage Ruth. She loves to meddle, but she's also always been a big part of my life. Our parents traveled constantly and when they were gone, Todd and I lived with Ruth. She had an incredible old house in Bel Air. The grounds were massive, two or three acres at least. We'd spend summers getting lost in the gardens. When we were at school, she'd show up for no reason, pull us out of classes and take us to the beach or Disneyland."

"That sounds nice." Doubt filled her voice.

"It was. You'll have to get to know her."

"I can't wait. At least the house will be cool if she asks me to visit."

"She doesn't live there anymore. She gave it to her daughter, who's the oldest of the two sisters and she passed it along to Todd."

Julie stared at him. "Todd lives in an old Bel Air mansion?"

"Does that change anything? Are you sorry he wasn't the one on the date?"

She laughed. "No. It makes him even more mock-able. What's a single guy doing with a house like that? It must be a museum."

"It is. Why do you find that so funny?"

"I don't know, but I can't wait to tell my sisters. Okay, my good manners are kicking in. How can I help?"

"You could set the table."

"Great. Show me where to wash my hands?"

"Sure."

He led her to the guest bathroom off the dining area. She glanced around at the white tile, marble floor and white fixtures, then returned her attention to him.

"You really need to work on saying no to your interior decorator."

"I know. It's a disaster."

"You could get snow blindness in here."

"If you think this is bad," he teased, "you should see the bedroom. It's all done in black and purple."

In less than a heartbeat, the entire mood shifted. Tension crackled between them. Ryan couldn't look away from her mouth, and the need to kiss her and hold her attacked him like a semiautomatic.

Julie opened her mouth, then closed it. "This is awkward," she said at last.

"It doesn't have to be." Although it nearly killed him, he took a step back. He'd given in to temptation at the law office and it hadn't furthered his cause. He tried never to make the same mistake twice. "See. All better."

It wasn't. At least not for him. The more he was with her, the more he wanted her, but for right now, he was going to ignore the heat and desire. He had to think long-term. He and Julie needed to establish a comfortable relationship so they could get to know each other. Then, when he'd softened her up, he would propose again. Because one way or the other, they were going to be married.

No child of his was going to be born without legally joined parents at his or her side. So he was willing to do whatever it took to convince Julie that she could take a chance on him—even not give in to the only thing they could agree on.

Sex.

Nine

This was her weekend for fancy lunches, Julie thought as she pulled into the circular drive in front of a large Beverly Hills estate. Yesterday she'd been at Ryan's for a surprisingly delicious meal and kind of pleasant conversation. She'd returned home to find a message from Ruth asking her to stop by this afternoon for a late lunch. The invitation had sounded very much like a command.

Julie had considered refusing for about three seconds, but then had called back to confirm. She wanted to get to know her grandmother. Ryan had painted a very different picture from the woman she'd met all of three times in her life. Maybe this visit would show her which Ruth was real.

She walked up to the impressive double doors and

rang the bell. A maid answered. When Julie gave her name, she was escorted through a foyer as large as her entire house, then into an equally large living room.

There were several sofas, close to a dozen chairs, tables, sideboards, artwork that belonged in a gallery and a man standing in front of the fireplace.

Her heart began to race even before he turned, so she actually wasn't all that startled to see it was Ryan.

Obviously he hadn't been briefed as to her arrival, she thought as he raised his eyebrows and smiled.

"Julie?"

The pleasure in his voice did something to her insides. Yesterday she'd had the chance to get to know the man. Despite everything, he was making a good case for himself. But seeing him so happy to see her gave him bonus points.

"Ruth asked me to lunch," she said.

"Me, too." He lowered his voice. "A command per-formance."

"Both of us together? Should I be worried?"

"I don't think so." He walked over and took one of her hands in his, then leaned in and kissed her cheek. "Regardless of why you're here, I'm happy to see you. Lunch yesterday was good."

So was he, she thought as she stared into his eyes and felt herself begin to tingle all over. His fingers were warm and her cheek burned from the light brush of his lips on her skin.

"I had a nice time," she admitted, suddenly wishing they weren't going to be disturbed.

She'd been involved with guys before, she'd even

been engaged, but she'd never had such a visceral reaction to a man.

"Oh, good. You're both here."

Ruth Jamison walked into the living room, her arms wide open, a smile on her carefully made-up face.

"Ryan, darling, how good of you to come." She hugged him and kissed him, then turned to Julie. "I still can't believe I have such lovely granddaughters."

Julie got her own hug and kiss, then Ruth linked arms with them both and led them to one of the sofas. When they were seated, she took a chair opposite.

"I know this was last minute," she told them, "so I appreciate you indulging an old woman."

"A sly old woman," Ryan said. "What's this all about, Ruth?"

"Does it have to be about anything?"

"Knowing you? Yes."

She smiled at him, then turned to Julie. "Don't listen to him. He'd have you believe I'm a terrible person, which I'm not. I'm very sweet. I'm also concerned. I heard that you went out with Ryan instead of Todd, dear. Is that true?"

The question was so unexpected, Julie didn't know what to say. How on earth had she found that out? Had Ryan told her? Ruth continued talking.

"While Ryan is a wonderful man and I'm desperate to see him settled as well, Todd's the oldest. He should be married first."

"He's older by a couple of months," Ryan said easily. "You don't really care about that sort of thing, do you?"

"Not generally, but this is different. This is family.

Your great-uncle had some very particular ideas and I intend to see them followed out. Todd marrying first was one of them. So what happened?"

"Ruth, this isn't your business," Ryan said gently, answering Julie's question about whether or not he'd been his aunt's source. But if he wasn't, who was?

"Of course it is."

Julie sensed danger ahead. She didn't want Ryan admitting the truth about their first meeting for a lot of reasons. She had the feeling that he was torn between wanting to answer his aunt and wanting to protect Julie. Rather than see where it would all go, she plunged into the conversation.

"I set up the date with Todd as you suggested," Julie said quickly. "Then he got tied up with some business and Ryan stopped by to tell me he was running late. He stayed for a drink and we ended up having dinner together."

Ryan shot her a grateful look. "That's right. Todd couldn't make it."

"I see." Ruth sighed. "So now what? Will you be going out with Todd?"

Oh, God. Because she needed more stress in her life? "No, I won't."

Ruth stared at her. "It's a million dollars, Julie. Do you know what you could do with that money?"

"I have a fair idea, but I'm good. Thanks for asking."

Later, when lunch was over, Julie and Ryan left together. When they stepped out into the cool afternoon, Julie turned to him.

"I can't figure out if she's just a crazy old woman or if she's the devil."

He shook his head. "Normally I'd take her side, but she's acting very strange. What's up with grilling us like that? And how the hell did she find out we had dinner instead of you and Todd?"

"I have no idea. Although I did think it was you."

"It wasn't."

"I got that."

He looked back at the house. "She's not usually like that. Maybe having granddaughters has gone to her head."

"We didn't come with any special powers. She seemed upset about me not wanting to go out with Todd. I'm going to have to warn Willow and Marina that she'll be coercing them next. Not that she'll have any luck with Willow. My sister is feeling very protective of me these days. The only thing she wants from Todd is the chance to yell at him."

Ryan stopped beside her car. "We've got a mess here."

"Oh, yeah. I totally blame you, by the way."

He chuckled. "How do you figure?"

· "You have really good swimmers. Otherwise I wouldn't be pregnant."

"I think it's all your fault."

She leaned against the driver's door and faced him. "Really? So guy-like."

"I'm a guy. It's your fault because you were smart and sexy and funny and you smelled good."

"The copier toner."

"Whatever. I didn't have a chance to escape."

"Did you want one?"

His eyes darkened with something that looked very much like desire.

She shivered. This was a dangerous game. She and Ryan were supposed to be in the "get to know you" stage of their relationship. Some people got to know each other *before* having a baby, but why be conventional?

Still, the smartest thing to do was pull back. To step away from the sexy man and drive home. But she couldn't seem to move, a little because the sexy man was so intriguing but also because she'd started to like him.

"It was a great night," he said. "You were amazing."

"You were adequate."

"Thanks."

She smiled. "You're very welcome."

He put his hand on her shoulder. A casual touch, she told herself. It meant nothing. So why was it suddenly so hard to breathe?

"We have to keep Ruth from finding out about the baby, at least for a while," he said. "In her present state, I'm not sure what she'd do with the information."

"The thought *is* a little scary."

"We also have a business meeting in a couple of days."

"I know. I put it on my calendar myself."

"Todd will be there."

"I have no words to describe my joy." Was it her imagination or was he moving closer?

"He's not such a bad guy."

"So you say." Ryan was definitely closer. Funny how she liked that.

"I'm not such a bad guy either."

She opened her mouth to say something back and he kissed her. He wrapped his arms around her, tilted his head and pressed his mouth to hers.

She meant to be affronted or at least crabby. Instead she parted her lips instantly, even as she pressed her body against his and clung to him.

Their tongues tangled in a sea of hunger and need. Wanting poured through her, making it impossible to care that they were in her grandmother's driveway. His kiss was hot and familiar and arousing and nothing mattered except that he never stop.

He ran his hands up and down her back. He cupped her rear and squeezed, causing her to surge against him. When she pressed against his hardness, she whimpered.

Oh, yes. That was exactly what she wanted—him hard and inside of her. Arms and legs tangling, bodies reaching, him filling her until she had no choice but to give in to the rising desire. Then they would—

No! She couldn't give in. Not again. Not until she'd figured out who he was and how she felt about him. Getting naked was a complication she didn't need.

It took all her strength, but she forced herself to step to the side.

"We have to stop," she told him, sounding more breathless than stern.

"No, we don't."

"I was just beginning to like you. Don't press your luck."

One corner of his mouth quirked up. "You like me?"

"A little. Maybe. Don't annoy me or the feeling will fade."

He grinned, then took a step back. "You are your own woman, Julie Nelson. You're definitely a hell of a ride."

The last time Julie had been at Ryan's office, she'd been too angry to pay attention to the elegant surroundings, but this morning she could appreciate the subtle blending of colors and the expensive but comfortable furnishings.

"Ryan should have slept with this decorator instead of the one who did his place," she murmured to herself as she walked into the reception area and gave her name to the woman behind the desk.

She was shown back to the conference room immediately. As her heels sank into the plush carpet, she reminded herself that this was strictly business. The kiss she and Ryan had shared a few days before was totally out of her mind. She was determined to be the best damn lawyer they'd ever had and to win them over. Ryan had offered three small companies to her firm. She'd done her research and knew there was a whole lot more where that had come from. She intended to walk away with it all.

She walked into the paneled conference room. Both men stood and smiled at her, but her gaze didn't see past Ryan. While she was aware that Todd was also in the room, she couldn't seem to convince herself that he mattered.

She stared into Ryan's eyes and he stared back and she would have sworn that time stood still. The ever-present need exploded, but she was practically used to that by now. She ignored the way her breasts got sensitive, and the sense of heat and dampness between her legs.

"Good morning," she finally forced herself to say.

"Morning." Ryan smiled. "It's really good to see you."

"Disgusting," Todd muttered.

Julie remembered where she was and forced herself to look away from the man who mesmerized her.

"Gentlemen." She put down her briefcase, refused an offer of tea, coffee or water, and took a seat at the small conference table. Todd and Ryan were across from her. "Let's talk business."

"We're ready," Ryan said.

She smiled at him, then turned her attention to Todd. "I don't think you are."

Todd, nearly as good-looking as his cousin, leaned back in his chair and shook his head. "What makes you say that, Ms. Nelson?"

"The way you run things around here." She'd decided on a blunt attack to set up her position, then she would drown them in facts to get them to agree with her. "You say you're interested in doing business in China, but your actions don't support that. You came to me for help with three very small businesses, but you're sitting on millions with your other holdings. I've been doing my research and you're getting screwed. Your deals are standard at best. At worst you're being taken. Your contracts don't protect you and your entire liaison staff is receiving kickbacks. I have the numbers to prove my position, if you'd like to see them."

She reached into her briefcase and pulled out several folders. Todd and Ryan looked at each other, then at her.

She continued. "I know I was offered a couple of

accounts as a peace offering and while I appreciate the gesture, I've decided I want all your business. Not for any reason other than you won't find a law firm that's better. You need more than advice, you need a partner. We don't farm out our contacts. They're all carefully screened. I speak with the Chinese liaisons myself. No one can claim a translation error."

"What the hell are you talking about?" Todd demanded.

She smiled. "I speak Mandarin."

"Yeah," Ryan said. "I guess I forgot to mention that."

"I learned from a neighbor," Julie said. "I spent several summers in China and did a semester of college there. I'm fluent."

"Interesting," Todd said. "If you'll excuse me for a moment."

Ryan watched his cousin walk out of the conference room, then he turned to Julie.

She looked amazing, but then she always did. Smart and sexy. How'd he get so lucky? If only he could convince her to marry him.

He had the feeling he was making progress, which was good. The more time he spent with her, the more he enjoyed her company, which was better.

"It wasn't mercy business," he said.

She shrugged. "Whatever. It was a very small slice of the pie."

"You want the whole thing?"

"Of course. Why would you think otherwise?"

"I have no idea. This would be a big deal for you. It's a senior-partner-level account."

"I actually know that." She smiled. "I'm capable."

She also understood how the game was played, he thought. "It would smooth things over with the partners when they find out you're pregnant."

"I know. It's part of my motivation, but not the biggest part." She leaned toward him. "Ryan, I'm really good. I know what I'm doing. If we were talking about Europe or Russia or South America, I wouldn't be pushing this hard. But I know this part of the world."

Her eyes were bright with excitement and conviction. Just once he'd like to see her eyes light up when she saw him. That would—

Whoa. Where had that come from? He wanted to marry Julie for the sake of his child. There were no other reasons. Sure, she was great and sexy and he wanted her, but this wasn't about having a relationship. He'd given up on those about six months ago. He was never risking his heart again.

Todd returned to the conference room with a Chinese woman. Ryan groaned.

"You're kidding, right?" he asked.

Todd ignored him. "Mrs. Lee, this is Julie Nelson."

Mrs. Lee bowed, then began to speak in what Ryan guessed was Mandarin.

Ryan narrowed his gaze. "You couldn't just trust her?" he asked Todd in a low voice.

"You wouldn't have trusted anyone else. If we're serious about giving her business, then she'd better be the right person." Todd frowned. "You used to be as much of a cynical bastard as I am. Don't tell me that's gone."

"Not gone," Ryan said as Julie and Mrs. Lee chatted about who knew what. "Shifted."

"Because of a woman?" Todd sounded incredulous.

Fortunately Mrs. Lee turned to him just then. "Her Mandarin is good and clear and she understands nuance." She smiled. "Her accent needs work."

Julie laughed. "I know. I try."

"You do very well."

Todd shrugged. "Okay, then I guess we have some things to talk about."

The conference door opened and Ryan's assistant stepped in. "Ryan, it's that call from the bank. The one you've been waiting for."

"Thanks."

He looked at Todd and Julie. "I have to take that. I'll be about five minutes. Try not to kill each other."

"We won't," Julie said cheerfully.

Ryan thanked Mrs. Lee for her assistance, then walked her out.

Julie glanced at Todd. "Speaking Mandarin is an odd thing to lie about."

"It's business."

"I understand." In his position, she probably would have done the same thing. Not that she was going to tell him that. "So, I have a question."

"Which is?"

"Your aunt offered a million dollars for me or one of my sisters to marry you. What's wrong with you that she would do that? Aside from the obvious."

She'd expected Todd to get angry, or at the very least, all puffed up and manly. Instead, he laughed.

"I'm starting to get what Ryan sees in you," he admitted.

"Which is charming but doesn't answer my question."

"My aunt has some interesting ideas about relationships. This is one of them." He leaned toward her. "I know you're still angry about that first date, Julie, but it's not all Ryan's fault."

"Oh, I know you're to blame, too."

"How refreshing. But that's not what I meant." He glanced at the door, then back at her. "Ryan had a rough time a few months ago. A complicated relationship."

As Julie had recently had one of her own, she understood how that sort of thing happened.

"Ryan's always been cautious," Todd continued. "We both have. But he met this woman and she seemed to be perfect. She wasn't interested in his money, she insisted on paying her way. She was a working single mother and he respected that. He was also crazy about her little girl."

Julie felt a twinge inside and this one had nothing to do with being enchanted by Ryan. Instead of heat, she felt cold and something heavy in her stomach.

She could do the translation for what Todd was so politely understating. Ryan had fallen madly in love with both the woman and her child.

Julie started to say she didn't care about that. She barely cared about Ryan herself. But somehow she couldn't seem to form the words.

"I met her and I thought she was great, too," Todd said. "I was a little worried because Ryan seemed to be more excited about being a father than being a husband, but I figured it would all even out. Things were getting serious when Ryan overheard her talking to her girlfriend. She said when she'd first gotten pregnant, she'd thought it was a disaster, but after her daughter was born, she'd discovered rich guys were suckers for cute little girls. They all imagined themselves playing daddy. The relationship itself was boring, but she would marry Ryan, wait two years, then leave and take a big chunk of cash with her. After all, he would have bonded with the kid, and he wouldn't want her to suffer."

The chill increased. Julie felt sick and for once it had nothing to do with her pregnancy.

"That's horrible," she murmured.

"And a whole lot more. Ryan was okay. He got out in time. But the experience battered him and made him feel stupid. Not something guys enjoy."

No one wanted to be an idiot, but in this case, Ryan had done nothing wrong. Sort of like her situation with Garrett.

"I can guess the rest," she said. "A few months later your aunt sprung her deal. Both of you saw me and my sisters as more of the same."

"That's it. I was telling Ryan about the situation and he offered to take my place."

"To teach me a lesson."

"It wasn't personal," Todd told her.

Funny how it had still hurt.

"I wanted you to know why he did it," Todd said. "You're having a baby with him. Ryan's a good guy. He made a mistake and he regrets it. That should count for something."

"It does," she said slowly. "But he still lied in a huge way. While I appreciate the situation the two of you are in, it doesn't give you the right to mess with innocent parties. I didn't do anything wrong. I wasn't her."

"He screwed up. Give him a break. If he'd known he was going to fall for you, he wouldn't have done it."

Fall for her? As in *fallen*? As in he *cared*?

Julie didn't want the words to mean anything, but they did. She wanted Ryan to like her and respect her, although why his opinion should mean anything, she couldn't say.

Ryan walked back into the conference room. "Sorry about that. So what did I miss?"

"We were just talking," Todd said.

They returned their attention to business and wrapped things up in an hour. Ryan walked Julie to the elevator.

"The partners will be happy," he said.

"I think they might even dance. I'm good at my job. You won't be disappointed."

"I know. How are you feeling?"

"Good. Still woozy a lot of the day, but I'm learning to live with it."

The polite conversation made her crazy. She really wanted to ask about what Todd had said. Had Ryan fallen for her and if he had, what did that mean? Was any of this real or was he still trying to convince her to marry him? And was marrying the father of her child be such a horrible thing?

"Have you told your family?" he asked.

"Everyone except my dad. I have no idea where he is." Not that she would waste any time tracking him down.

"I haven't told my parents. They're in Europe. They don't get back to the States very often, but you'll meet them when they do."

She had a vision of her very pregnant self waddling to meet a couple straight from the pages of *Town & Country* magazine.

"Great," she muttered.

"I should meet your family, as well," he said.

"What?"

"Don't you want me to?"

It was a trick question. No, she really didn't want him to meet them. It would be awkward and strange and…awkward. But to refuse when they were having a baby together?

"That would be fun," she managed to say.

"I'm free this weekend."

How lucky for her. "Okay. Um, sure. I'll, ah, set something up."

"Good."

He leaned forward and kissed her lightly.

There was none of the passion or power of their last kiss, but it still rocked her to her toes. He straightened and smiled.

"Until this weekend, then."

"Sure. I'll be the one with the pickle cravings."

Ten

The house was modest at best, one in blocks and blocks of starter homes. Ryan parked and tried to take in the fact that while he'd grown up in a world of wealth and privilege, Ruth's granddaughters had grown up here.

He climbed out of his sports car and walked to the front door. Julie already had it open. She leaned against the door frame.

"Are you braced? You should be braced."

"Your sisters can't be that bad," he told her as he approached. "I'll be fine."

"Silly, silly man." But she was smiling as she spoke.

He slipped past her, then turned around and kissed her. She didn't react, but he caught the sudden surge in heat and tension. They might have other issues, but connecting sexually wasn't one of them. Maybe he'd been too quick when he'd decided that his plan would progress better if they weren't physically involved.

"My mom's at work," Julie said when he straightened. "She's in charge of a low-cost vaccine clinic one Saturday a month, but she'll be by later. In the meantime I have my sisters here to grill you—ah, keep you entertained."

He chuckled. "They can grill me. I can handle it."

"So you think."

The morning was warm, with the promise of a hot day—the kind that pops up every now and then in the fall. Julie wore some kind of filmy, lacy blouse, with a loose neckline and tiny sleeves that left her arms bare. Instead of jeans, she had on a skirt that sort of floated around her calves. Her feet were bare, her hair hung loose. She looked like a wanton fairy princess.

Ryan stopped in the middle of the living room. A wanton fairy princess? What the hell was wrong with him?

"This way," Julie said from a few feet in front of him. "No backing out now."

"I don't plan to."

She led him through the kitchen and out into a backyard that was far more paradise than he ever would have expected. There were plants everywhere, a big patio with a table and chairs at one end and a barbecue and fire pit at the other. There were candles and things that spun in the wind and gauzy, hanging fabric that served no purpose he could see.

There were also two women, both blond and blue-eyed, with Julie's features and identical "you're going to have to prove yourself" expressions.

"My sisters," Julie said. "Willow and Marina."

Willow was fairly petite, delicate and pretty. Marina was the tallest of the three sisters, and a beauty as well. Great gene pool, he thought. At least their kid had a fighting chance at being cute.

"Nice to meet you," he said and smiled. "Julie's told me a lot about you."

"Did she mention how we wanted to take you down?" Willow asked. "Not just you, either. I still want to march over to that house and give Todd Aston a piece of my mind. You wouldn't happen to have the address, would you?"

Ryan cleared his throat. "I, ah, the backyard looks great. There are so many plants. You have a very special place here."

"Not exactly a smooth change of subject," Marina said, her arms folded over her chest. "I doubt you're seriously interested in the landscaping, but in case you're not just jerking us around, Willow's the one who does all that."

Ryan held in a groan. They were going to be a tough crowd.

Julie urged him to sit and took the chair across from his. "Willow can grow anything. She's into herbs and all things organic. She has a line of candles that are very popular in some of the health-food stores and she writes a comic strip."

He looked at Willow. "Impressive. Do you have any of your comics here? I'd like to read one."

She picked up a slim magazine from the glass-topped table and tossed it to him.

"About eight pages in," she muttered.

He flipped through the pages of the publication. There were articles on organic gardening, an essay on surviving cold-and-flu season and a pull-out diagram on how to get the most from your compost.

Then he saw the small six-panel comic. There were two squash talking about a shoe sale. Judging from the bows on their heads and their high heels, they were girl squash. Okay, then.

He read the panel and forced himself to chuckle at the end, even though he had no idea what the punch line meant.

When he'd finished, he said, "That's great. Is this syndicated?"

"In a couple of small-town newspapers. The major publications aren't interested in organic humor."

"They're missing a growing market."

Willow eyed him as if trying to figure out if he was patronizing her. He was about to launch into a conversation on the phenomenal growth of the organic market—one of their start-ups was in the business—when Willow and Marina stood.

"We'll go get snacks," Marina said.

When they'd left, he turned to Julie. "I don't get it," he whispered, waving the magazine. "Explain it to me."

She leaned close. "I can't. I don't get it, either. Maybe you have to be a vegan to understand, I don't know. For a while I thought maybe Willow's comics just weren't funny. But she's in more and more magazines all the time, so it must be me. Well, and Marina and my mom."

"And me," he said.

She smiled at him and he grinned back.

The sisters returned.

"Mango lemonade," Willow said, handing him a glass.

Marina put a plate of cookies on the table.

Mango lemonade? He took a sip. It wasn't half-bad.

Marina and Willow sat back down.

"Have you ever been married?" Willow asked.

"No."

"Engaged?" This question came from Marina.

"No."

"Any children, other than the one Julie is carrying? And please don't say 'not that I know about.' That just makes guys look stupid."

So the grilling had begun. "No other children."

They were thorough. They covered everything from his relationship with his mother to asking about his financial situation and whether he paid his taxes on time. Through it all, Julie sat back and watched him, as if judging him by his answers.

He was good with that. He had nothing to hide. So he answered their questions without stumbling, right up until Willow said, "How could you be so weasely to lie about who you were with the express purpose of hurting that person?"

The patio got very quiet.

He started to say he hadn't thought Julie would get hurt, but that didn't sound right. Saying he'd assumed she was incapable of emotion wasn't smart. He could explain how he'd been hurt badly and why he'd felt the need to get back at someone. Only Julie hadn't been the one to hurt him. In the end, he went with the truth.

"I was wrong," he told Willow. "There's no excuse for my behavior and I won't try to make one."

Marina and Willow looked at each other, then at Julie. Willow gave a slight shrug.

He felt that something important had just happened, but he wasn't sure what. At times, women were a serious mystery.

"When we were little, Julie was really bossy," Marina said. "Especially to me."

Julie groaned. "I was not bossy at all. However, our mother worked and someone had to be in charge. I was the oldest."

Willow leaned toward him. "Bossy. Big time."

"I'm ignoring you," Julie said as she stood and walked around the table so she could pour herself a glass of the mango lemonade. But instead of sitting back in her original chair, she settled in the seat next to his.

He made the mistake of glancing at her bare feet when she crossed her legs. Dear God—she painted her toes bright pink and wore a toe ring. It was about the sexiest thing he'd ever seen.

Focus on the plan, he reminded himself. He had a plan to get Julie to marry him. For the sake of the child.

But right then, the child didn't seem very real. All Ryan could think about was that he liked Julie and her sisters and that their cozy house was a home in ways his had never been.

"You didn't buy this, did you?" Julie asked as Ryan pulled up in front of a massive Beverly Hills estate. The wrought-iron gates swung open, exposing a three-story house, manicured lawns and lawn art. Who owned lawn art?

"I grew up here."

"What?" She stared at him. "You lived here? With your parents? You told me to dress casual. You said we'd probably be getting dusty. I can't meet your parents looking like this."

She was in jeans and a T-shirt she'd been about to toss in her "donate" bag. She hadn't bothered with makeup or washed her hair.

"They're not here," he said as he parked by the front steps that led to the huge double front door and turned off the car. "They're in Europe. I brought you here so we could go through the attic. I thought there'd be some stuff there you'd like."

Her panic faded. "Oh. Okay. An attic sounds intriguing." She climbed out of the car and looked around. "Very stylish. Nothing like my house."

He moved next to her and unlocked the front door. "I liked your house. It was warm and homey. This place isn't."

They stepped inside and he pushed buttons on a keypad that had been concealed behind a panel. Julie took in the soaring ceilings, the hardwood floors and impressive artwork. Hey, and this was only the entryway.

"No staff?" she asked.

"There's a live-in housekeeper. Today's her day off. I told her we were stopping by but that she didn't need to be here. We have the house to ourselves."

Ryan led the way up a grand, curving staircase, then along a hallway flanked by bedrooms.

"So how big is this place?" she asked. "Ten thousand square feet?"

"I think closer to fifteen."

"That's a lot of vacuuming."

He grinned. "I wouldn't know."

"It would be a full-time job. I can't believe your parents own this place and they're never here."

"They like to travel."

Julie rubbed the long, smooth banister. "My sisters and I could have had a lot of fun on this thing. Who would need to go to a theme park? You did good with them, by the way. Did I mention that? You nearly won them over."

They reached the landing and he looked at her. "I did win them over. There's no *nearly* about it."

"Cocky, aren't we?"

"With cause."

Danger signs flashed all around them. She knew better than to be charmed but she couldn't seem to help herself. The guy was pretty cool.

At the end of the hallway, they took another, slightly less impressive, staircase to the third floor. Instead of more bedrooms, there were several large, open areas, giving the space a loft-like feel. Windows let in massive amounts of light.

"I love this," she murmured. "It makes me wish I was a painter or something creative. Wouldn't this be a great studio?"

"Todd and I played up here when we were young. We had the whole floor to ourselves."

"Kid heaven."

Tucked in the corner was a third set of stairs. These were narrow and steep. Julie followed Ryan up and found herself in a musty attic.

It was something out of a PBS original movie—with exposed beams, furniture covered with sheets and dusty windows. There were boxes everywhere, along with trunks and hanging racks.

How was it possible that she and Ryan had grown up less than twenty miles from each other and had lived such different lives? How could this world be real?

Ryan walked around and pulled off a few sheets. "Todd and I spent a lot of time up here. We dug through nearly everything. Most of it was pretty boring for a couple of boys, but I remember…"

He crossed the dusty wood floor and moved a few boxes, then beckoned her forward.

"I know how you feel about ultra modern. Is this more your style?"

He'd promised her a surprise. She hadn't been sure what to expect, but it hadn't been a beautiful carved bassinet.

She dropped to her knees and sucked in a breath as she touched the smooth finish. Angels and hearts and flowers adorned the piece. It was a little battered, but mostly incredible.

"Oh, Ryan. It's stunning."

"I'm glad you like it. We can get it refinished or painted or whatever. There's a matching dresser." He sat down beside her. "This stuff is maybe a hundred and fifty years old. There's no changing table, but we could get one made. The same with a crib."

"That sounds great. How did you know I would love this?"

His dark gaze settled on her face. "I just knew."

She would have guessed he was the kind of guy to give traditional, expected gifts, but she was wrong—and happy to be so. Not that she would be keeping the pieces. They were family heirlooms. But she would be delighted to use them while the baby was young.

"You're unexpectedly thoughtful," she said. "Thank you. These are amazing."

"Good. I've been doing some reading online. About babies. They need a lot of stuff."

"It is hard to believe something so small needs so many accessories."

He leaned against a chest and stretched out his legs in front of him. "Can you feel anything yet?"

She touched her stomach. "Just faint queasiness. No movement. It's going to be a couple of months before that."

"You're barely showing."

"I have a tummy." She'd been about to say he should see her naked, but that would lead them to places probably best left unvisited.

"When are you telling the partners?" he asked.

"Soon. I have to. There are a lot of details I'm going to have to work out, but I'll make it work. It's so strange. Until I found out I was pregnant, my career was the most important part of my life. I lived for work. I was determined to get ahead, no matter what. A baby is really going to mess that up and I can't seem to mind."

"You won't be making the decisions alone," he told

her. "I'll be participating. I'm going to be a present parent, Julie. I want to be there for my child."

He sounded determined and intense. "I'm good with that," she said. "We can both interview prospective nannies."

She'd meant it as a joke, but he grimaced.

"I had a nanny."

As big as the house was, and as much money as his family had, she shouldn't have been surprised. Yet she was. "Interesting. Was she nice?"

"I had several and they were all fine. My parents preferred to avoid the hands-on aspect of raising a kid. They took me when they traveled, but we weren't ever together. I don't remember them taking me places themselves or sharing meals with me. I had my own suite at the hotel, with my nanny, sometimes Todd, if his folks were along."

That was so not the picture of his childhood she'd expected. She'd imagined something far more perfect and loving.

"Sounds lonely," she said.

"Sometimes it was. I did better as I got older and was able to get out on my own. I could meet other kids. Once I was in school, I was safe, except for the summer. We were always flying off somewhere."

Julie remembered her childhood summers as long, lazy days spent in the garden. She and her sisters would invent elaborate games that took days to play out.

"Todd helped," Ryan continued. "We were there for each other. Like you and your sisters."

"They're important to me," she agreed.

"I want more for our baby, Julie. I want our child to

know we're both there, that we both care. I want us to create a family. I want the family I never had."

He sounded both determined and painfully sad. She ached for the small boy who'd had so many things and yet so little of what really mattered.

"I don't think we can go back and give you that family," she said. "I know I don't want to re-create mine. But we can build something new, that works for us."

He nodded. "I'd like to try that." He looked at her. "Does your dad know about the baby yet?"

She wrinkled her nose. "I certainly haven't told him. If my mom spoke to him recently, then she might have mentioned it."

"You don't like him. I can hear it in your voice."

"I can't forgive him," she admitted. "He hurts her over and over again. I know she has some responsibility in that—she keeps letting him come back. I just wish she would dump him once and for all and find a good guy. But she claims to love him."

"You don't believe her?"

"I don't think love is supposed to hurt that much."

He reached out and took her hand. Of course there was the usual array of tingles and tightening and desire. Julie had the feeling she would always experience that when Ryan was around. But there was also something different. Something warm and comforting. As if she could trust him to be there.

Not likely, she told herself. But it was nice to pretend.

She shifted so she sat crossed-legged. "I was engaged once," she said quietly. "His name was Garrett and he was very charming. We met in law school."

"I hate him," Ryan said lightly.

She smiled. "That is a testament to your excellent taste." She shrugged. "I keep looking back, trying to figure out where I went wrong and no matter how many times I go over the material, I can't figure it out. I don't see what clues I missed. I like to think there weren't any, but who knows. Anyway, we started dating, we fell in love, or so I thought, we got engaged."

She looked at Ryan. "He was already married. His wife, a very sweet young woman, lived back in New Mexico with her family. She was working two jobs to pay for his education. They'd decided it would be cheaper for her to stay with them, while he got a studio apartment here and went to UCLA."

Ryan's hold on her hand tightened slightly. He swore.

"My thoughts exactly," she murmured, fighting emotions she didn't want to feel again. She'd been a fool, it was over, move on. "So we were engaged and planning a post-graduation wedding. The only reason I found out about his wife was that she won the lottery." Julie managed a smile. "Nothing big—about thirty thousand dollars. But it meant she could move out and be with him and only have to work one job. She showed up without warning. All three of us got a really big shock."

Ryan pulled her close. She stiffened, then relaxed into his embrace. She knew her life was better with Garrett out of it, but still, the hug felt good.

"I don't know what he planned to do," she said, her head resting on his shoulder. "Was he going to be a bigamist? Was he going to wait until the last minute to tell me? Was he going to disappear? I don't know and I didn't stay long enough to find out. I got the basic facts and I took off."

She closed her eyes. "I hated how stupid I felt. Even more than missing him and still loving him, the stupidity of it all killed me. I'd always thought of myself as so smart, and yet he'd fooled me totally."

"He was a bastard and a liar. I'm sorry you had to go through that."

She opened her eyes and looked at him. "Yes, well, now you can see why your little stunt might have pushed a button with me. Besides the obvious reasons."

He grabbed her by the shoulders and shifted so that he could look into her eyes. "I've apologized. I think you believe me. So here's what I want to know—are you ever going to be able to let it go?"

Interesting question. It all came down to whether or not she wanted to. Was she willing to accept that he'd had momentary bad judgment, that it hadn't been personal and that if he could take it back, he would? How long did she want him punished?

"I'm getting closer," she admitted. "A lot closer. But you need to back off on the whole getting-married thing."

"Hey, I mentioned it once. And for the record, you seriously overreacted."

"Oh, please. It was a terrible way to propose. Besides, once was enough."

"You don't want to get married?"

She wondered what he was thinking. Was he relieved that she'd refused or had he really meant that they should get married? She wasn't sure which she wanted it to be.

"Eventually," she said. "But because I want to, not out of duty."

"A romantic. I never would have guessed."

"Not a romantic. I just want to find someone special. The right guy for me."

He dropped his hands to her knees. "So what's he like, this right guy?"

"I don't know—I haven't met him yet."

"So you're available."

What? "Are you planning to set me up with one of your friends? Do you have someone in mind?"

"Of course," he said as he leaned close. "Someone charming and successful and very good-looking."

She could feel his breath on her face. Anticipation swept through her. "Let me guess. Someone we both know?"

"Uh-huh. Me."

"Why am I not surprised?"

But he didn't answer, which was fine with her. Because he kissed her instead.

Eleven

Ryan wrapped both arms around her and slowly lowered her to the floor. At the same time, his mouth claimed hers in a kiss that stirred her to her soul. She felt weak and hungry, powerful and on fire. Her body ached for possession and her heart wanted to open and accept this man inside.

Only her brain wasn't sure if, after all this time, he could be trusted. Still, right now Julie was far less concerned about trust than feeling his hard body pressed against hers. Sometimes, you just had to go with the moment.

His tongue swept leisurely through her mouth, teasing, exploring, exciting. He lowered one hand to her hip and slid his palm across the slight swell of her belly before climbing higher. Her muscles clenched in anticipation of him touching her breasts. Her breath caught in her throat until the weight of his palm settled on her curves.

She was more sensitive than she'd been before, she thought as he lightly brushed against her nipples. More sensitive, but in an amazing, connected, oh-God-I-might-come-right-now sort of way. Sensation shot through her, burning down to her fingers and toes. Between her legs, she felt both heat and dampness.

He broke the kiss and smiled down at her. "I used to dream about this when I was in high school. A sexy woman in my attic. I'd nearly forgotten about it, but suddenly the memories are very clear."

"Did it ever happen?"

"Not until today."

"So I'm about to fulfill an erotic adolescent fantasy."

"That would be my preference."

She pretended to consider the matter. "It's interesting, I suppose. So what exactly did you want to do to this mystery woman?"

His smile turned wicked. "Everything."

She shivered in anticipation. "Can you be more specific?"

"Of course."

But instead of telling her, he bent down, pushed up her T-shirt and pressed an open-mouthed kiss to her belly. After unfastening her jeans and pulling them open, he used his tongue to tease her belly button.

Even as her insides clenched and she fought against begging to be taken right then, she managed to kick off her shoes so he could tug her jeans down and toss them aside. Her T-shirt followed.

He supported himself on one elbow. With his other hand, he traced patterns on her rib cage. "Your skin is so soft. I used to wonder what it would be like to touch a woman. How she would be different. I read a lot, I listened to other guys talk, I imagined, but I wasn't prepared for the softness."

She liked knowing he hadn't always been so experienced and together. "So how fast was that first time?"

He chuckled. "An eighth of a second. I just wanted to be inside and finally do it. I didn't appreciate the subtleties until later."

"Subtleties?"

He unfastened the front hook of her bra with a quick movement of his fingers. "The way a slow build can make the end result even better. How I can know what you like by the way you react to my touch."

The air in the attic was warm, yet goose bumps broke out on her skin.

"If I do this…" He slipped his index finger across her tight, sensitive nipple.

Instinctively, she closed her eyes and arched her body toward him, silently asking for more.

"See," he murmured. "You react."

He bent low and took the same nipple in his mouth. The combination of wet heat and gentle sucking made her gasp. Ribbons of need flowed down her body. She ran her fingers through his hair, then squeezed his shoulders as he shifted to her other breast.

He circled her, then drew her deeply into his mouth.

He trailed one of his hands down her stomach and slipped his fingers under her panties into the waiting dampness below.

She parted her legs for him and let her eyes sink closed. Yes, she thought hazily. This was what she wanted.

He explored her, dipping a single finger inside of her before settling on that one hypersensitive spot. Then he began a dance designed to send her screaming into her release. But just as she settled in to enjoy the ride, he straightened and removed his hands.

Her eyes popped open. "Are you all right?"

"I'm fine." He began unfastening his shirt.

Oh, good—live entertainment, she thought as she slipped off her panties, then stretched back out and watched Ryan undress.

He worked efficiently, first shrugging out of his shirt, then kicking off his athletic shoes and tugging at his socks. He moved to his jeans next. Her gaze focused on the impressive bulge there. All that for her?

"It must be difficult to have your interest out there," she said as he stepped out of his jeans and colored briefs. She reached toward him and stroked his arousal. "There's nothing subtle going on. Women can pretend interest we don't feel. Guys can't."

"We're more honest," he said as he knelt next to her and bent down to nibble on her neck.

"You're not more honest," she said, her voice breathless. "But it could get really awkward to be hard in a situation where you don't want to be. Plus, we always know if you come. Women can fake it."

He raised his head and looked at her. "I'd know."

"I'm not so sure. Some women fake it really well."

"I'd know," he insisted stubbornly, then he smiled. "We'll test your theory. Go ahead and try to fake it. See if I'm fooled."

He shifted so that he was between her thighs, then parted her gently and gave her an intimate kiss that took her breath away.

She had no time to prepare, no time to brace herself for the arousing sensation of lips and tongue against her body. She went from "this is nice" to "I need this or I'll die" in less than a heartbeat. Her body was on fire, her muscles trembled and all she could do was lie there and feel what he was doing to her.

He moved slowly at first. Exploring, tasting, making her shake and gasp and moan. He circled her center with his tongue before gently sucking.

She wanted to scream out her pleasure. She wanted this to never, ever end. Instead she parted her legs as wide as she could and pushed herself against him.

He moved faster against her—stroking up and down, over and over again. He slipped a finger inside of her, moving at the same pace, the same intensity, pushing her forward until she had no choice but to let herself fall.

Her climax began deep inside of her as muscles began to clench and release in a rhythm as old as time. She gave herself up to the waves of pleasure, calling out his name, surrendering everything.

Her orgasm went on and on for what seemed like an hour. When the last waves faded away, he shifted and plunged inside of her.

The unexpected penetration thrilled her. She held on to him, wrapping her legs around his hips, pulling him in closer. He filled her over and over, driving deeper.

She came again, only this time he was with her. He stiffened and groaned. She took all of him, wanting it to always be like this—the connection. The perfect moment.

He opened his eyes and looked down at her. "You weren't faking it."

She gave a strangled laugh. "I know."

Later that week, Julie stopped by her mom's house. It was nearly nine, but she'd been caught up in a brief that had taken way too long to pull together. Still, her mother had said any time before ten was fine, and Julie took her at her word.

She parked in the driveway, then walked to the back door, knocked once and pushed it open.

"It's me," she called, before being led inside by the delicious smell of baking chocolate. "What is that?"

Her mother looked up from the pan in front of her and smiled. "Perfect timing. The brownies are cool enough to serve. I know you want one."

Julie's stomach growled. "I'm starved."

Her mother glanced at the clock on the stove. "Didn't you eat dinner?"

"No. I meant to, but I got busy. Then I came straight here. I'll grab something when I get home."

"Julia Marie Nelson, you know better than that. You're pregnant. You can't go around skipping meals."

Great—talk about feeling as if she were eleven again. "Mom, I know I need to eat regular healthy meals. I've been doing really well. But tonight got away from me. I'll do better."

"All right. Save the brownie. I'll make you something for dinner, first." Her mother walked over to the refrigerator and stuck her head inside. "I have lasagna."

"Yours or Willow's?"

"Willow's." A vegetarian, all the time. "I'd kinda like something with meat. Anything else?"

"Some roast from last Sunday. How about a sandwich and a salad?"

"Sounds great."

While her mother removed various items from the refrigerator, Julie collected a plate, napkin and a knife until her mother shooed her away.

"Go sit. I'll bring you the sandwich."

"Mom, I'm pregnant, not dying."

"I know, but sometimes I like to baby my girls."

As Julie's feet hurt and her back was a little achy, she wasn't about to push the point. Instead she claimed a seat at the island—a tiny version of the massive one in Ryan's ultra-modern kitchen.

Ryan. Just thinking about him made her smile. She hadn't seen him since Sunday when they'd made love in the attic of his old house. That unexpected event had been followed by an evening at her place, which had turned into a very nice sleepover. When he'd left just before sunrise, she'd had to hold back the need to say "we should do this again." Not because she didn't want to but because everything was confusing.

Her life had changed so completely, so quickly. She

didn't know what was happening with him, or what she wanted to happen.

"Have you been to a doctor?" her mother asked.

"I have my first appointment next week. I'll be seeing the same ob-gyn I've been using. I like her and I've heard she's great through the whole pregnancy."

"Is Ryan going with you?"

Interesting question. "I don't know. I haven't asked him."

"You should," her mother told her. "He seems like a nice young man." Naomi stopped and winced. "Tell me I didn't just say that. Nice young man? I sound like my mother. Worse! I sound like *her* mother."

Julie laughed. "It's okay. I won't tell anyone you've entered your dotage."

"If I'm in my dotage, what does that make your grandmother?"

Julie hesitated, then said, "Not the nicest person on the planet."

Naomi finished with the sandwich. She opened a plastic container and dumped a prepared salad into a bowl.

"What do you mean? I thought you liked your grandmother."

"I don't know her," Julie said, hedging. "She's a little scary. At first I thought the whole 'marry my nephew' bit was charming, but when I really go over what she said, it's creepy. She can't control us with money."

"I don't think she was trying to. It was her way of connecting two families. If she'd simply asked you to meet Todd, would you have agreed?"

"Probably. Just to be nice."

Of course without the million dollars on the line, Todd wouldn't have freaked and Ryan wouldn't have stepped in. So she would have gone on her date with Todd, been pleasant and it would have all ended very differently. How long would it have been, under those circumstances, before she'd even have met Ryan?

She was surprised by the panic and regret that seized her. As if not meeting Ryan, not getting involved with him, would be something to grieve.

She didn't want to think about that so she turned to a slightly safer subject.

"Grandma had Ryan and I stop by recently," she said. "She wanted to know how I'd ended up on the date with Ryan instead of Todd and did I have plans to go out with Todd in the future."

Her mother sighed. "She always did love to meddle."

"Apparently. I don't know what has happened to her in her life and I'm sure deep down she's a lovely person, but I have trouble accepting what she did to you. You were seventeen, Mom. She threw you out and turned her back on you."

Naomi set the food on the island. "It's not her fault. I disappointed both my parents."

"Disappointed, yes. Became an ax murderer, not so much. You're her only daughter. I can see having a big fight, not speaking for a while, but twenty-six years? That's excessive."

"Fraser was a difficult man," Naomi murmured.

"He sounds like a tyrant. But here's what I don't get. From what I've seen, Ruth is a really strong woman. If that's right, she could have stood up to him and insisted on seeing her child." Julie touched her mother's arm. "You did an incredible job with all of us. I don't regret anything about my childhood. But it makes me crazy that you had to work so hard and suffer so much and they were only a few miles away, ignoring you and us."

"I wouldn't have taken anything from them."

"I'm not talking about money. You could have used someone to talk to or with babysitting so you could have an evening by yourself."

Her mother smiled. "I love my girls and I'm very happy with my life."

"I'm glad. I just don't understand your mother. I can't figure out if she's a victim or the devil."

"She's not the devil."

"Maybe. But she does have to take responsibility for actions, or lack of action. We all do."

"Even me?" her mother asked quietly.

Julie looked at her. "What do you mean? Leaving with Dad? Mom, you were seventeen. You're allowed to be impulsive."

"I didn't mean that so much as what's happened since then. I know you don't approve of me."

Julie set down her sandwich. Suddenly she wasn't so hungry. "Mom, I love you and I only want you to be happy. It's not my place to approve or disapprove. You've made your choices."

"Which you don't understand."

Julie shrugged. "I don't. He's my father and I love him." Sort of, she thought. "But I don't forgive him. He has no right to appear and disappear from our lives on a whim. Family is about more than that. Family is about taking responsibility."

"He loves us."

"He has a funny way of showing it," Julie muttered. "I can't stand it when he shows up and you're so happy. I know what's coming. Sure enough, he sticks around just long enough for us all to believe in him again, then he's gone. He breaks your heart over and over and you let him."

"He's a good man and a good father."

"He wasn't a good father to me."

"Oh, Julie. You're going to have to learn to be a little more tolerant of people and their flaws."

"What? A flaw is leaving toothpaste in the sink or being chronically late. Abandoning your family over and over is a little more than a flaw. You're so great and pretty and there are wonderful men out there who would love to have you in their lives. They would treat you like a princess."

"I just want to be Jack's wife," her mother said sadly. "I wish I could make you understand that loving someone doesn't mean you get to change him. You accept the good with the bad."

"His bad is too big for me," Julie told her.

"But not for me."

Julie thought about pointing out that there were other women when her father left, but why state the obvious and cause pain?

"Sometimes loving someone means forgiving over and over," her mother said. "You pick what you can live with. I can live with this. I have to. He is, as your sister would say, my destiny."

"Oh, please." Julie gave a strangled laugh.

"I'm serious. Don't you think I've tried to get over him? When you were younger, after he'd stayed nearly three months and I was sure that this time he'd changed, but he hadn't, I decided I wasn't going to do that anymore. I wasn't going to get my heart broken again. So I started dating. I went out with several men. One of the relationships even got a little serious."

"Mom! You wild woman. You never said anything." Julie hadn't had a clue.

"I didn't know how it was going to work out and I didn't want you girls to be disappointed by another man. I thought it best to wait until I was sure."

"I'm guessing it didn't work out."

Her mother shook her head. "I wanted to love him, but I couldn't. For better or worse, I love your father. I've learned I would rather be missing him than trying to love someone else."

Julie didn't know what to say to that. Talk about a sad choice.

"He's older now," her mother continued. "He'll be settling down soon. And when he does, it will be here. With me. We'll grow old together."

Julie tried to understand, but she couldn't. "Wouldn't you have rather had a whole life instead of just the end of his?"

"I'm content, Julie. You may not understand that, but you need to accept it. This is what I want."

"I know, Mom. I'll let it go."

"I hope you can. I hope you can find someone who makes you happy. Is that person Ryan?"

"I don't know," she admitted.

"He's the father of your child," her mother said gently.

Julie looked at the woman who had been so important to her for so long. "You'd like me to just forgive him and move on," she said. "You'd like to see us married."

"I'd like to see you happy. I worry about all my girls. Marina, because she leads with her heart. Willow, because she finds men who need rescuing, and once they're healed, they move on to someone else. And you because—"

"Because I'm stubborn and difficult and don't trust easily."

"You because you've been hurt and you don't trust yourself to pick a good man."

"Same thing." Julie poked at her salad.

"Does Ryan make you happy?" her mother asked.

"Sometimes. Maybe. He's not so bad."

"I'm sure he'll want you to be in charge of his ad campaign if he ever runs for public office," Naomi teased.

Julie smiled. "You know what I mean. If I pretend we met a different way, then he's amazing. He's smart and caring and yeah, I like him."

"You can't change the past."

"I know, but occasionally I try to argue with it."

Her mother grinned. "Does that work?"

"Not as well as I'd like. I just wish things were different."

"Events can't be undone. People are who they are. He's a good man, and the father of your child. You're starting to care about him. Isn't all that what you want?"

"You'd think so," Julie said with a shrug. "But in my gut, I'm still afraid he's lying or holding back or there's some big secret and when it all comes out, my heart will be broken again."

"Getting involved is a risk. For what it's worth, you survived Garrett."

"True." Julie drew in a breath. "But getting over Garrett was a lot easier than it should have been. I'm terrified I won't be able to get over Ryan."

"You're falling for him," her mother told her.

"Apparently. And I don't think I want to."

"Can you stop those feelings from growing?"

Not if they continued to spend time together, Julie thought, remembering the previous weekend. It wasn't just about the sex. It was about the way they talked together and laughed together. It was how he made her feel, and how much she wanted to trust him.

"I refuse to fall in love," Julie said.

Her mother nodded. "I thought you might decide that. On the one hand, I think you've made an incredibly sad choice. On the other hand, I don't think anyone, even you, has that much control. Ryan isn't going away. He will always be the father of your child and in your life. Can you resist him forever?"

Julie already knew the answer to that was no. So if falling for him was inevitable, why was she struggling so hard to resist him now?

Julie made a note on her pad. She needed a couple more citations and then she'd be ready to write up her brief. There was a knock on her open door. She glanced up.

"Come in," she said to the short, older man standing there.

He was dressed in jeans and a sweater, nothing fancy. He looked especially nondescript.

"Julie Nelson?" he asked.

"Yes."

"Julia Marie Nelson?"

She didn't like people using her full name. It reminded her too much of when her mother was mad at her. "May I help you?"

He handed her a thick envelope. "You've been served." With that, he was gone.

Julie stared at the envelope, then opened it. The accompanying letter was from a law firm in the next high-rise over. As she scanned the contents, she felt her entire body grow cold. Her heart cried out in protest, her brain muttered, "I told you so," and her chest tightened until it was nearly impossible to breathe.

Ryan was offering an official prenuptial agreement and a proposal of marriage valid only after the baby was born and his paternity was proven by DNA testing. If she refused either the proposal or the test, then he would sue her for custody of the child. Permanent and total custody. He would have her or she would have nothing.

Twelve

Julie stormed into the offices of Aston and Bennett, ignored the receptionist and stalked down the hall to Ryan's office. She found him on the phone.

He looked up when she entered and smiled. Dammit all to hell if she didn't feel a kind of quiver. Crap, she thought grimly. It was all crap.

She jerked the phone from his hand and hung up, then tossed the papers in his face.

"How could you?" she demanded, her voice loud and angry, but not nearly as loud and angry as she felt on the inside. "How could you? I trusted you. I believed you. That's what kills me. I was starting to think I'd been wrong about you. That I'd misjudged you. That it had all been a simple mistake. But it wasn't, was it? You were your own true self that first night we were together. You were a snake then and you're a snake now."

Ryan grabbed the papers and stood. "Julie, what are you talking about?"

"That." She pointed at the papers. "You think you've won, but you are sorely mistaken. I'm a better lawyer than you'll ever be able to hire. You won't get anything, you hear me? You're going to lose. You're going to lose big time and then you're going to have nothing. Not this baby and not me. Let me be clear. I will never marry you. Never. The next time I see you, we'll be in front of a judge. I will eviscerate you. I will leave you broken and bleeding and then I'm going to kick you while you're down. You're a lying bastard and I can't tell you how much I wish I'd never met you. I can't believe I thought I was in love with you."

With that, she turned and left.

Ryan stared after her, stunned by her attack. He couldn't think, couldn't feel, couldn't understand what was going on. He opened the envelope and read the paperwork. Horror filled him.

"No," he said between clenched teeth. "Julie, no. I didn't do this."

He went after her, but it was too late. The elevator doors had closed and she was gone.

Now what? How could he explain he hadn't done this? And who the hell had?

But he already knew that answer. He walked into Todd's office and closed the door.

"What are you doing?" he demanded. "This is crazy.

Why would you go behind my back? Do you know how you've screwed up things?"

Todd frowned and reached for the papers. He scanned them, then groaned. "Oh, God, Ryan, I'm sorry. I never meant for this to go out to her. Did Julie see this?"

"Based on what she just said to me, yeah. She was served earlier today. What the hell were you thinking?"

"I wanted to protect you. I went to see our lawyer after she came by for the first time. Before I knew anything about her. I just told him I wanted you protected and that you wanted to marry her, which I thought was crazy." Todd looked at him. "I didn't do any more. He wasn't supposed to do anything but draw up papers. I swear."

Ryan believed him. Todd was looking out for his back. If their situations had been reversed, Ryan might have done exactly the same thing.

But the plan had backfired. Instead of covering his back, the papers had ripped him open and destroyed any chance he had of getting Julie ever to trust him. He was empty inside and he had a bad feeling that later he was going to long to feel nothing more than empty. Because when reality hit, it was going to be grim.

"We hired a shark on purpose," he said with a meager attempt at lightness. "He just made a kill."

"He wasn't supposed to kill you."

"Killing Julie isn't a good idea, either."

She'd said she loved him. He'd wanted to hear those exact words from her…just not in that context.

"You'll make her understand it wasn't you," Todd said. "Tell her. Hell, I'll tell her."

"Why would she believe either of us?" Ryan asked wearily. "I wouldn't. Would you? I lied to her when we first met. I lied and I hurt her. I've been working my ass off to regain her trust and now this. She's going to think it was all a game."

"You love her," Todd said. "You can't just let her go."

"I won't," Ryan said. "I'll win her back…just as soon as I figure out how."

Julie lay curled up on her sofa. She'd been unable to face the thought of going back to work, so she'd come home. She'd managed to maintain something close to control until she'd been in the door, then the tears had poured down her face and the sobs had choked her throat.

She cried so hard, she felt she would soon break in two. This couldn't have happened. Ryan couldn't have lied about all of it…but he had.

Garrett's betrayal had been impossibly harsh and unexpected, yet after her initial shock, she'd thought only about getting as far away from him as possible. But now, even though she hated Ryan and wanted him punished and humiliated, she was just as upset at the thought that she would never see him again.

"I'm mentally uns-stable," she said, her voice breaking on another sob. "I need professional help."

Someone knocked on the door.

She stiffened, then covered her mouth with her hand. She wasn't going to answer that. Odds were it was Ryan and she wasn't interested in talking to him now or ever.

The bell rang, followed by more knocking.

"It's Todd. I know you're in there, Julie. Your car's

in the driveway and the hood is still warm. You just got here. Let me in. We have to talk."

"We don't have to do anything," she yelled as she stood and glared at the door. "You're just like him. You're a complete bastard. Go away or I'm calling the cops."

"I'm not leaving. You can let me inside, or I can yell your personal business loud enough to keep the neighbors talking for weeks. Let me in. You'll want to hear what I have to say."

"I doubt that," she muttered and put her hand on the lock. Let him in? Why not? There was nothing he could say that would change her mind.

She opened the door.

Todd stepped inside. He looked enough like his cousin to make her stomach clench. She fought against tears, not wanting to cry in front of him. Kind of pointless, she admitted to herself. She already looked like a wreck.

"Why are you here?" she demanded. "Go away."

"I just got inside," he told her. "Hear me out. Then you can kick my ass."

If only, she thought bitterly. Why hadn't she learned some karate method? Hearing a couple of bones snap right now would be very satisfying.

He pointed at the sofa. "May I sit down?"

"No."

"You're pregnant and upset. You should sit. I'll stand."

"I'm fine." She folded her arms over her chest. "Start talking."

Todd drew in a breath. "Okay, but once I start, you have to let me finish. No interruptions."

She glared at him. "Excuse me? Who do you think

you are? You don't get to set the rules here. Your cousin screwed me, in more ways than one. You don't get to set anything, you jerk."

"Fine. I'll talk fast. It wasn't Ryan, it was me. Ryan didn't know I went to see our lawyer and he doesn't know I'm here now. I have the bill to prove my point— about the lawyer, not about me being here now. It shows I consulted with our attorney for over an hour about you two. I was trying to protect my cousin because he was in no position to protect himself. All he could think about was how he'd blown it with you. He felt horrible about what had happened."

It hadn't been Ryan? Julie walked to the sofa and sat down. Was that possible? Was this an elaborate trick?

"Ryan would never do that," Todd told her. "I wouldn't now, either, but I didn't know you then. I thought you were just in it for the money and that you'd tricked Ryan into getting you pregnant."

"I'm flattered."

"I apologize, but there have been plenty of women who would do just that. At the time, I needed to make sure you weren't one of them. Look, Ryan is the only real family I have. I would do anything for him. I just wanted to make sure he was okay. But I messed up. You're blaming him and because of what I did, you don't trust him. It's not him, Julie. He's a great guy. I'm the bastard. Hate me."

What she hated was how much she wanted to believe him. Based on what she knew about Todd, this was exactly something he would do in the name of protecting his buddy. But was it possible Ryan knew nothing about it?

"It's just too much," she said quietly. "All of it. The ride's been too much, too fast. I need time."

The front door opened and Ruth stepped inside.

"You simply leave your house unlocked?" the older woman asked as she shut it behind her. "Not a very safe way to live." She glanced at Todd. "You're an unexpected visitor."

Julie rose to her feet. "So are you, Grandmother."

"I know. I phoned your office, but your assistant said you'd gone home ill. I came to check on you, and my great-grandchild."

Okay, and the hits just kept on coming. "You know about the baby?"

"I know everything. Well, not everything. I didn't know you were going to go on that date with Ryan instead of Todd. If so, I would have stepped in. Todd is the oldest and I did so want to see him married first."

Julie's head was spinning. She had just enough brain power left to invite Ruth to sit before she collapsed back on the sofa.

"How did you know about the baby?" Julie asked.

Ruth glanced at Todd, who still stood in front of the sofa. "Are you lurking, dear boy? Don't lurk."

He took a step back.

Ruth turned to Julie. "The young woman who comes to my house and does my nails has a sister who works in a law firm. It's the same one where Ryan and Todd do business. I've used her from time to time, just to keep in touch with their business. Those boys tell me nothing. She told me about those papers. A little harsh, perhaps, but they get the job done."

Julie didn't know what to react to first. The fact that Ruth was spying on her own nephews—which really put the whole marry-Todd-for-a-million-dollars thing in perspective—or that a secretary in a law firm was giving out privileged information.

She looked at Todd who looked as angry as she felt.

"I'll have her fired," he said.

"Of course you will," Ruth said breezily. "I've already arranged for her to have a wonderful new job, so run off and take care of things while I talk to Julie."

Todd hesitated. Julie sensed that he was actually going to stay to make sure things were all right with her.

"I'm good," she told him. "You can go."

"If you're sure?"

She nodded.

Todd left, closing the door behind him. Julie turned to her grandmother.

"You've been busy."

"I need to stay involved with my family."

Julie realized she'd had enough meddling and controlling and lies and subterfuge to last five lifetimes.

"Okay, Grandma, here's the thing," she said. "You can't do this. You can't spy and trick people. That isn't how you treat family and it's not any way to get family to want to be around you. I know you're old and I should respect that, but I can't forgive you for what you did to my mom. She was seventeen and you threw her out."

Ruth stiffened. "Your mother chose to leave. It was her decision and she knew the consequences."

"You made her choose. My father was the first man she ever loved—apparently the only man she'll ever love—and you made her take sides. What did you expect her to do?"

"Her duty."

"Isn't it a mother's duty to love her children no matter what? But apparently that's not your way. I guess in your world, people get to mess up one time, and then you turn your back on them. Well, here's a news flash. Don't bother caring about me because I'm going to mess up big time. I'm going to disappoint you. It's inevitable. I'd rather you knew that now and got out of my life. That would be easier. I don't want to care about you only to find out there are strings and conditions on your affection."

Ruth paled. "How dare you talk to me this way?"

"Someone has to. Why do you hold on so tight to Ryan and Todd, yet you let my mother go so easily? Are you..." Julie opened her mouth, then closed it. Of course, she thought as the truth dawned on her.

"You're sorry about what happened," she said slowly. "You have nothing but regrets where she's concerned. But you never knew how to make it right with her—either because of your pride or your husband. You were afraid she'd reject you again, so you didn't try. But you had Ryan and Todd and they almost made up for it. So you clung to them, torn between loving them and needing to control them so they wouldn't disappear the way your daughter had."

Tears filled Ruth's eyes, but her expression remained stern and disapproving. "I have no idea what you're talking about, but I can see your mother did a terrible job in raising you. You're rude and unprofessional."

"Unprofessional?" Julie actually smiled. "This is a personal conversation. I don't have to be professional."

"Fine. Be what you want, but know this, young lady. You're having my great-grandchild and you will be marrying Ryan Bennett."

"No, she won't."

Julie looked up and saw Ryan had stepped into her house. He ignored her and turned to Ruth.

"Julie isn't going to do anything she doesn't want. No one is going to make her. Not you, not me, not anyone. I want her happy—that's *all* I want. If she can be happy with someone else, then I'll step aside."

Julie stared at him, not totally sure she believed him, although she was disgustingly thrilled to see him.

"You're being ridiculous," Ruth told him, her voice sharp. "I won't stand for this."

"Then take a seat, because it's what's going to happen."

"But you love her," Ruth said. "I can tell because you've never been this stupid about a woman before. It's not like you to be a fool."

He looked at Julie and gave her a rueful smile. "I don't care. I just want you not to hurt anymore. I can't seem to stop screwing up."

She stood and took a step toward him. Seeing him felt so right. She could believe that Todd had made a mess of things, and now Ruth was here, butting in. Did any of that matter? Weren't she and Ryan the ones who had to make the decision about what was right for them?

Then Ruth's words really sank in. Love? Did Ryan love her? Her soul brightened at the thought. Her heart beat faster. Could he? Did he?

"Propose," Ruth instructed. "Propose now and we'll have this business done."

"No," Ryan told her. "I won't marry Julie. It's the only way I can make sure she's happy."

"What?" both women asked together.

He grabbed Julie's hands and stared into her eyes. "I made you cry. I never want to do that again. I never want you to doubt me or us or my motives. I only know one way to do that. Not to marry you. Because that's what I've wanted this whole time. Us, together. At first it was about the baby, but now it's more. It's about you."

He drew in a breath. "I hate how we met. It was the best and worst night of my life. By the time I realized what I was doing and how great you were, it was too late to start over. Then you were hurt and angry and I knew I'd blown it. But the baby gave us a second chance. You *had* to deal with me and I thought maybe, with time, you'd start to like me. Only then I proposed and that set you off again and I was back where I'd started."

The words were magic. They were warm and loving and everything about this moment was so perfect, except maybe for Ruth being there.

"I love you," he said as he smiled at her. "I love you and I will never make you do anything you don't want to do. We'll co-parent, I'll buy the house next door. You just tell me and I'll be there. I swear, Julie. I had nothing to do with those papers. I would never, ever do that to you."

"I know," she said breathlessly. "I know. I just reacted and then I didn't know how to un-react when Todd told me the truth."

"Todd was here?"

"I haven't had this many people through the house since my last Christmas party." Her eyes burned with more tears, but these were happy ones. "I believe him and I believe you, Ryan. When I hurt so much, thinking you'd lied and tricked me, I realized I love you, too."

Julie braced herself for Ruth's instant criticism that if they loved each other and were having a baby together that getting married seemed the sensible solution. Only there wasn't a sound.

She turned and saw the older woman had slipped away. The front door was closed and she and Ryan were alone.

"I wouldn't have thought she was that sensitive," she admitted.

"Me, either. Todd, Ruth and I are going to have a long talk about her way of keeping in touch."

"She's alone and holding on too tight," Julie said, surprising herself and possibly him. "Be kind."

"I will." He kissed her fingers. "I do love you."

"I love you, too." She tilted her head and fought a smile. Suddenly she felt as if she were channeling Ruth. "Which does beg an interesting point. We *are* having that baby together."

"Yes, we are."

"Traditionally, couples prefer to be married."

"I've heard that." He released one of her hands to touch her face. "Are you saying you'd be *willing* to marry me? Despite everything?"

Julie smiled. "I'd actually be honored."

He pulled her close and kissed her. She wrapped her arms around him and hung on. He was the kind of man who would always be there for her, just as she would always be there for him.

"We're going to make a great team," she murmured.

"Go us," he said as he nibbled his way down her neck.

"I'm serious. We'll be one of those wildly efficient couples who has everything done on time. We'll have to move, of course. This place is too small and your condo, well, I can't even imagine living there. We'll need a house."

He raised his head and smiled at her. "My parents would give us theirs if you wanted."

"Maybe just the attic. I had a good time there."

"I always have a good time with you." He kissed her again. "We actually owe Ruth for bringing us together. If we have a girl, we could name her after her great-grandmother."

Julie winced. "Tell me you're kidding."

He drew her toward the bedroom.

"Ryan! Wait! We're *not* naming our daughter Ruth. I won't have it. Do you hear me? What happened to whatever I want? What happened to me being in charge?"

"I never said you were in charge." He tugged her blouse out of her skirt.

"It was implied."

"This is a partnership. Equal votes."

"Fine. As long as mine counts just a little bit more."

He laughed, then kissed her again and suddenly she didn't care about being in charge or baby names or anything but the amazing man who had claimed her heart and changed her world forever.

* * * * *

New York Times *bestselling author*
Linda Lael Miller
is back with a new romance featuring
the heartwarming McKettrick family
from Silhouette Special Edition.

SIERRA'S HOMECOMING
by Linda Lael Miller

On sale December 2006,
wherever books are sold.

Turn the page for a sneak preview!

Soft, smoky music poured into the room.

The next thing she knew, Sierra was in Travis's arms, close against that chest she'd admired earlier, and they were slow dancing.

Why didn't she pull away?

"Relax," he said. His breath was warm in her hair.

She giggled, more nervous than amused. What was the matter with her? She was attracted to Travis, had been from the first, and he was clearly attracted to her. They were both adults. Why not enjoy a little slow dancing in a ranch-house kitchen?

Because slow dancing led to other things. She took a step back and felt the counter flush against her lower back. Travis naturally came with her, since they were holding hands and he had one arm around her waist.

Simple physics.

Then he kissed her.

Physics again—this time, not so simple.

"Yikes," she said, when their mouths parted.

He grinned. "Nobody's ever said that after I kissed them."

She felt the heat and substance of his body pressed against hers. "It's going to happen, isn't it?" she heard herself whisper.

"Yep," Travis answered.

"But not tonight," Sierra said on a sigh.

"Probably not," Travis agreed.

"When, then?"

He chuckled, gave her a slow, nibbling kiss. "Tomorrow morning," he said. "After you drop Liam off at school."

"Isn't that…a little…soon?"

"Not soon enough," Travis answered, his voice husky. "Not nearly soon enough."

Harlequin® Historical
Historical Romantic Adventure!

Loyalty...or love?

LORD GREVILLE'S CAPTIVE

Nicola Cornick

He had previously come to Grafton Manor to be betrothed to the beautiful Lady Anne—but that promise was broken with the onset of the English Civil War. Now Lord Greville has returned as an enemy, besieging the manor and holding its lady prisoner.

His devotion to his cause is swayed by his desire for Anne—he will have the lady, and her heart.

Yet Anne has a secret that must be kept from him at all costs....

On sale December 2006.
Available wherever Harlequin books are sold.

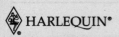

HARLEQUIN®

American ROMANCE®

IS PROUD TO PRESENT

COWBOY VET
by Pamela Britton

Jessie Monroe is the last person on earth
Rand Sheppard wants to rely on, but he needs
a veterinary technician—yesterday—and she's the
only one for hire. It turns out the woman who
destroyed his cousin's life isn't who Rand thought
she was. And now she's all he can think about!

"Pamela Britton writes the kind of
wonderfully romantic, sexy, witty romance
that readers dream of discovering
when they go into a bookstore."

—*New York Times* bestselling author
Jayne Ann Krentz

Cowboy Vet *is available from*
Harlequin American Romance in December 2006.

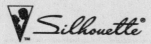

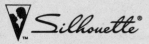